When she checks in, someone

KILLER LIBR

Praise for the first novel in Mary Lou Kirwin's
mystery series featuring transatlantic librarian-sleuth
Karen Nash

"How can you not buy this cozy debut with its catchy title?
Mary Lou Kirwin succeeds at creating a winning heroine
whose amateur sleuthing efforts make for a fun, gentle puz-
zler with a touch of love."   —*Library Journal*

"Literary allusions, from Winnie the Pooh to Ian McEwan,
distinguish Kirwin's captivating debut from the common run
of cozies."   —*Publishers Weekly*

"This engaging cozy has it all—English bookshops, flower
shows, dotty sisters, plenty of surprises—along with an engaging premise for a continuing series."   —*Booklist*

"A charming debut for Mary Lou Kirwin. . . . I hope this
author has more books coming, and soon."
                                             —*Suspense Magazine*

"Kirwin weaves literary gems into the story that will keep
the reader jumping to keep up. Add a new love interest to
mix into the stew and there is something for everyone in this
book."   —*Single Titles*

Death Overdue

Mary Lou Kirwin

G

GALLERY BOOKS

New York   London   Toronto   Sydney   New Delhi

G

Gallery Books
A Division of Simon & Schuster, Inc.
1230 Avenue of the Americas
New York, NY 10020

First Gallery Books trade paperback edition November 2013

GALLERY BOOKS and colophon are registered trademarks of Simon & Schuster, Inc.

For information about special discounts for bulk purchases, please contact Simon & Schuster Special Sales at 1-866-506-1949 or business@simonandschuster.com.

The Simon & Schuster Speakers Bureau can bring authors to your live event. For more information or to book an event contact the Simon & Schuster Speakers Bureau at 1-866-248-3049 or visit our website at www.simonspeakers.com.

Manufactured in the United States of America

10 9 8 7 6 5 4 3 2 1

Library of Congress Cataloging-in-Publication Data is available.

ISBN 978-1-4516-8466-7
ISBN 978-1-4516-8467-4 (ebook)

I'd like to dedicate this book to all the librarians
who have shown me the right book at the right time.
Many thanks.

The books were arranged rationally, thematically, al-phabetically, and dust-free: this last was the only sign of housekeeping in that austere place.

A. S. Byatt, *Possession*

"When I used to read fairy tales, I fancied that kind of thing never happened, and now here I am in the middle of one!"

Lewis Carroll, *Alice's Adventures in Wonderland*

One never knows when the blow may fall.

Graham Greene, *The Third Man*

Acknowledgments

Many thanks to Janet Cox for vetting my take on the Brits and Pete Hautman for his hugs and help always.

ONE

 (decorative flourish)

Arranging the Books

Sitting on the floor surrounded by books, I realized I had never been happier in my life.

The sun streamed in the open window of Caldwell's library, which had been a bedroom in his B and B at one time but was now filled with floor-to-ceiling bookcases holding row upon row of amazing books. Not in perfect order. Not in terrifically bad order, but I wanted to organize them to my satisfaction. I'm a librarian, and I know how these things should be handled.

Caldwell was running errands, and I was glad to have both some meaningful work to do and time to myself to think over the last few months of my life—how things had changed. Caldwell and I had fallen in love under rather dire circumstances and, for both of us, we needed some time to just be together and see if what we were feeling for each other had legs, as they say.

There were inherent problems in our relationship: he lived in London, I lived in Sunshine Valley, Minnesota. The plane trip took a good eight hours if you were lucky and then there was the jet lag. Neither of us was a spring chicken; rather we were in the prime of our forties. My previous boyfriend had dumped me and then died rather tragically. Caldwell had started the B and B with his previous girlfriend, who had later run out on him, leaving him to fend for himself and make breakfast for the guests. But that was quite a few years ago. We were both recovering from these upsetting and unreliable relationships.

I hadn't thought I would retire from my job as a librarian for some years yet, but Caldwell was ready to jump with both feet into running a bookstore (or as he was constantly reminding me in British English, a "bookshop") here in London. He wanted it to be called Nash and Perkins, our two last names; therefore, he wanted me to be involved in the running of said shop. He felt we would make very good partners. He had hinted at wanting to make us more than simply business partners. I had the same thoughts, but was being cautious.

I had come over to London about a week ago to try this new lifestyle on for size. Over the years I had accumulated many weeks of vacation time, having taken them so infrequently. I had asked for two months off to help Caldwell get his life and his books organized and to see if we wanted to take these next steps together.

Since Caldwell had been scouting around for the perfect shop, word had gotten out of his intentions and was already stirring up interest in his collection. While he collected a great variety of books, he was specializing in children's books. One of our guests was a well-known book collector, Bruce W. Hogsworth. Bruce wanted desperately to see Caldwell's library, but so far Caldwell had put him off—just not ready to let go of any of his books.

At the moment, I was trying to decide how to arrange Caldwell's nonfiction, whether to stick with strict library methodology or to be more loose, more intuitive about what books to put next to each other. For example, Caldwell puts all the books about Canterbury, England, together even if they should be shelved apart because some are about its geography and others are about its history.

This can grate on me. By nature, I am not intuitive. I believe everything has its proper place. But along with thinking of making a major change in my life—like moving to England and opening a store and living with a man I love—I was trying to be a little more relaxed about all things.

For instance, I was learning to eat dinner later. I was used to eating promptly at six. That's when Caldwell might start thinking about dinner. We went out to eat more than I was used to.

And he often bought books because they were handsome, while I tended to focus on their monetary worth.

When I arrived, Caldwell had told me that he had found a wonderful first edition in very good condition. "I'm still checking out whether I'm right about this book. If I am, it alone could finance the start-up of our business."

"Will you be able to sell it?" I asked, knowing that he could get quite attached to certain books.

He hesitated before saying, "I think so."

He hadn't told me what book it was or shown it to me yet. I trusted him. He would reveal it to me when he was ready. I knew it could well be secreted away in the very room I was sitting in, but I wasn't going to search for it. I was content to let things unfold as they would.

I wanted to share this lovely, quiet moment with someone, and so I called Rosie, who worked with me as a librarian and who, even though she was a couple decades younger than me, was my best friend. In Minneapolis, it was early in the afternoon. She would be home unless her new beau, Richard, had taken her out to see an early movie.

"Hey," she said when she answered the phone.

"Hey, yourself. How are things in Sunshine Valley?" I was

feeling so good I nearly sang this question to the tune of "How Are Things in Glocca Morra?" and I don't even like the song.

"The usual. Nancy, our favorite librarian, griped all day long about how much work you've left us with and how your replacement shouldn't be allowed to pump gas, let alone touch a book."

Nancy was the head librarian and took her work very seriously. Not that Rosie and I didn't, but we tried to have fun too. "I'm glad to hear nothing has changed."

"But you've changed. You sound positively glowing."

"You can tell that over the phone?" I asked.

"Yes, your voice is all full of bubbles."

"Well, it feels good to be here," I admitted.

"With Caldwell," she added.

"Yes, with Caldwell. Guess what I'm doing."

"Sitting in the back garden eating some crumpets."

"No, I'm sitting on the floor of the library, which is really just this room that used to be a bedroom that Caldwell has filled with shelves, and I'm organizing his books."

"That's enough to make any librarian happy."

"And sometimes I'm not even putting them according to the Dewey decimal system."

"Oh, you are a wild thing. So things are going pretty good. Are we going to lose you to this Svengali?"

"Maybe. I'm just taking it a day at a time, until I have to decide."

"Which is in seven weeks," she reminded me. "Oh, there's the doorbell."

"What movie are you seeing tonight?" I asked. Seeing movies was about all she did with Richard—but they both loved it.

"We're staying in tonight and watching *Casablanca*."

Which made me want to sing "A kiss is just a kiss." "Toodles," I said.

"Ta-ta." Rose signed off.

The only fly in the ointment of my utterly perfect moment and heavenly day was the decision I had to make—did it make sense for me to completely give up my life and step so deeply into Caldwell's? How well did I really know the man? Why did I have to lose so much to gain him?

I was trying hard to pay attention to what *felt* right to me. After Dave's horrible and untimely death, I had seen a therapist for a few months. At first, when she would ask me how something made me feel, I literally didn't know what to say. I hardly knew what she meant. Cold and hot I could distinguish, but how I felt emotionally about an event was a real struggle for me to ascertain. I had a few episodes of sobbing and laughing hysterically in the therapist's office. I guess you call those breakthroughs although at the time they felt more like breakdowns.

As I sat in front of a wall of books, trying to decide whether to put so-and-so's book on British history in the historical books, where it belonged, or in the section on royalty, next to a book on Princess Diana, where it might also find readers, I was also working on simply feeling happy, letting this emotion wash over me in waves.

How odd to have to practice feeling happy.

Just at the moment when I thought I had nailed it— when happiness flooded over me like a warm and powerful rain shower—the doorbell rang. Little did I know that answering it would completely blow my happy world apart.

TWO

⤫

Knock, Knock

When I opened the door, I saw the back of a tall, blond-haired woman, who was wearing the loveliest fawn suede shoes I have ever laid eyes on. Shoes that one wanted to reach out and pet. I refrained.

The woman turned, and she was equally good-looking from the front. She was not young, but she was elegant and willowy and very well kept up. She looked at me like I was a marmot, and a hoary one at that. I'm not even exactly sure what a marmot looks like, but that was how I felt, especially in comparison to her.

The tall, blond woman twisted her lovely lips, then undid them and asked, "Who are you?"

Assuming that she was a guest who had been expecting Caldwell to answer the door, I told her, "Oh, this is Perkins B and B, I'm just the . . ." What exactly was I? *Girlfriend* didn't sound like quite enough, but I certainly wasn't his fiancée yet. I didn't work for him, but then I did, by choice. I continued, "I'm just helping out."

"Doesn't Brenda still do that?" she asked.

Brenda was Caldwell's housekeeper-assistant, who had recently moved into a small room on the first floor. She had been with him forever, but only worked part-time. This woman must be a regular guest to know of Brenda—she worked odd hours and didn't make her presence known much.

"Yes, Brenda is still here, but not at the moment. I'm helping Caldwell with other things." I was being circumspect because Caldwell and I had decided to keep mum about the possibility of the bookshop. We didn't want to scare the current or future guests away.

The blond woman craned her long neck and looked past me into the house. "How nice that he's been able to keep the place going."

Thinking that was a rather odd comment to make, I asked her, "Do you have a reservation?"

"Yes, as a matter of fact, I do. Remulado. It's under the name of Alfredo Remulado."

She looked like neither a Remulado nor an Alfredo, but I stepped back to let her into the entryway. She left her single suitcase on the steps, and I realized she expected me to serve as bellboy. I reached out for the case and was surprised by how heavy it was. Then I saw that the thing was made of some sort of metal. Thank goodness it was on rollers.

"When do you expect him back?" she asked as she walked down the hallway toward the garden room.

I followed, the suitcase trailing me like a robotic dog, squeaking as its little wheels turned. "Shortly," I said. "But I'm sure your room is ready if you'd like me to show you the way."

"Oh, I'd rather sit down here and wait. I want to see his face when he finds out I'm here."

As she sank into the couch in a languid movement, I perched the suitcase next to her, in case she might need anything out of it. "Can I get you something to drink?"

She looked at me as if seeing me for the first time, then said, "Oh, you're American, aren't you?"

The contempt with which she asked this question was unavoidable, and I stepped right smack into it. "Yes," I answered bravely, then added, "Minnesota."

"Wherever that is."

I had learned not to try to explain precisely where my home state could be found—people didn't know where it was because they didn't care. So I made my usual statement, "Not far from Chicago."

"I know Chicago," she said, then nodded as if that was way enough information. Then she said, "Some tea would be nice. I haven't had a cuppa in years."

Caldwell didn't usually let me make the tea. He said I hadn't quite yet perfected the British way of brewing it. I didn't argue. I liked having him make the tea, and I figured it was such a small thing to disagree about. But I had watched him carefully and now followed his steps. Heat the water in the kettle until it just comes to a boil, rinse the teapot with the hot water, a swirl will do. Then measure a teaspoon for each person consuming the tea and one for the pot. I figured I might as well join her, as I deserved a break from book arranging. I threw in another tea-spoon in the hopes that Caldwell would return shortly.

On a tray I placed not the super-good teacups, but the second best. No need to kowtow to her superiority. A pitcher of milk and a bowl of sugar, two spoons, and I was off.

Taking care not to spill the tea, I navigated the hallway. When I entered the back room, I found the woman standing and staring out the window at the garden.

"It's not quite what it used to be," she said sadly.

"So you've stayed here often?"

"You could say that," she agreed as she sank back down into a chair.

I didn't want to serve the tea just yet. Caldwell was very particular about letting it brew five minutes, and it had only been three.

"Well, let me introduce myself. I'm Karen Nash. A librarian. This is my second visit to England."

She smiled. "So I suppose you're a real booklover?"

"You could say that," I responded. My hackles were rising. There was something about this woman that I didn't care for. She was acting as if she owned the place.

"My name is Sarah. Like Bernhardt. But everyone calls me Sally. Sally Burroughs."

I wanted to tell her that Sarah Bernhardt was not tall and willowy but short and curvaceous—really resembling me more than her—and that the esteemed actress was certainly never languid.

Sarah continued, "I've been living in Italy for the past few years, but I'm thinking of coming back home."

She gave me a sharp look. I wasn't sure why.

I poured her a cup of tea and offered the milk and sugar, but she shook her head and held out her hand. This was when I first noticed her bright red nail polish, a color very few women should wear. I wasn't sure she was one of them. I poured myself a cup and added just enough milk to slightly lighten the tea. I couldn't help but compare her nails to my fingernails, which were unvarnished and slightly dirty from dusting all the books.

We sipped in silence for a few minutes.

"How's Caldwell?" she asked.

This question made me smile. I was sure he had never been happier in his life—or that's what he told me every day. "I would say he's doing quite well."

"That's good. Caldwell has always been such an amiable sort. I've missed him quite a bit."

"Yes, *amiable* is a good word to describe him." In French the word means "lovable," and I certainly found him that.

"I can't wait to see him," she said.

I wondered how well she did know him. She seemed to act like they were old friends, and yet I had never heard Caldwell mention her. Not that he talked a lot about all the guests he had hosted over the years.

Just then I heard the front door open. I knew it was Caldwell as soon as I heard him walking down the hall. He clomped a bit, in a way I loved.

"We're here in the garden room having some tea," I said as he got closer.

"Great," he said as he entered the room, looking first at me and then at Sarah.

As I watched, his eyes grew, his mouth opened, the books in his arms fell to the floor. He just couldn't resist buying more books. He took a deep breath and said in a voice that bespoke horror, "Sally, whatever are you doing here?"

In that instant, everything she had said so far made horrible sense: how she had missed him a bit, and wondering where Brenda was. I knew this was his old love, the woman who had deserted him, left him with the B and B to run.

Sally looked up with a slight smile playing on her lips. "Why, Caldwell, I've come back to claim all that was mine."

THREE

What's New?

Caldwell didn't have a chance to ask Sally what she meant because the doorbell rang again. He walked down the hallway to answer it and left me alone with his ex-girlfriend.

"He hasn't changed," Sally said.

"Did you expect him to?" I asked.

"Well, it's been a long time. I thought he'd look older, but he looks good. And he seems happy. Funny how time goes so fast. But I have missed this place. And, of course, Caldwell."

I hated hearing her say that, but didn't know how to claim Caldwell as my own. "Who's Alfredo?" I thought to ask her.

She waved her hand as a tall, dark, younger man entered the room followed by Caldwell. "Here he is. Alfredo Remulado, who claims descendancy from the House of Savoy. This is Caldwell, of whom I have told you so much. And this is Katy, and I'm not sure what she's doing here."

"Karen," Caldwell spit out. "Her name is Karen, and she is my . . ."

I waited to hear what he would call me.

He continued, ". . . dear friend, who I'm hoping will also become my partner."

I couldn't help but be a little disappointed that he hadn't declared his love for me, but then he wasn't like that, nor was I.

"Partner in what?" Sally asked. "In crime?"

"In books," he said. "We're going to sell the B and B and open a bookshop. We've got it all planned."

"Oh, I see. Her being a librarian and all, that makes good sense."

During all of this time Alfredo stood at attention, focused on Sally. When there was a pause, he turned to me and finally spoke. "Hello, charmed to meet you," he said with a fairly heavy Italian accent.

He did ooze charm—from his dark swath of hair that fell just so over his forehead, to his full lips, to his suitably wrinkled but excellently cut linen jacket. He too was wearing elegant shoes. It appeared to be true what they say about Italian shoes—that they are the best in the world.

"Tea?" I offered.

Caldwell plunked down in a chair and said, "Yes, please." I could tell he was terribly thrown by Sally's presence because, as I've said, normally he would insist on making it himself.

Alfredo looked around the room. "I wouldn't mind an aperitif. It is almost the hour."

I poured Caldwell a cup of tea with a splash of milk, which is how he likes it. Sally held out her empty cup. Reluctantly, I poured her a refill, while I thought of dumping the tea into her lap.

Caldwell went to the cabinet in the corner and pulled out a bottle of vermouth. He poured a small glassful and handed it to Alfredo. Then he walked around the table and sat next to me.

When we were all seated, Caldwell finally asked, "Sally, what in God's name are you doing here?"

"I told you, Caldwell darling. I'm here to claim what I left behind. You didn't think I had gone away forever?"

"I had only hoped," he mumbled, then said more clearly, "And what exactly do you think you can claim? My recollection is, after you took the money, you left everything remaining to me, for better or worse."

"Oh, that was just temporary."

"Seven years is temporary?" he asked.

"Yes, in the scheme of things it is."

He fell silent. I wanted to step in and fight for him but knew he had to do it on his own.

Steps sounded coming down the stairs.

Caldwell lifted his eyes up with a fighting gleam in them and said to Sally, "Well, I have a surprise for you too. Guess who's here."

We had only two other guests—Bruce, the book collector, and Penelope Winters, who had arrived late last night, after I went to bed. All Caldwell had said about her was she was an old friend. I hadn't thought to ask him any more.

Now, as Penelope stood in the doorway, I saw the resemblance between the two women, although Penelope was a smaller, rounder version of Sally, not nearly as dramatic and with a warmer, more genuine smile. That smile dimmed, then vanished when she spotted Sally.

Caldwell whispered to me that they were sisters, which I had already guessed. I assumed one of them had married, thus the different last names.

"So you did come back. I wasn't sure you would," Penelope said to Sally with a note of steel in her voice.

"Well, dear sister, I'm glad to see you too. Why shouldn't I come back? It's a free world."

"What do you want this time?" Penelope asked.

"Only what I am due. After all, it's my fair share," Sally said with a toss of her long blond hair.

"What do you think you're due?" Caldwell jumped into the conversation as Penelope came to stand by him and put a hand on his shoulder.

"I want the B and B back. I'm so happy that you've kept it going. I must say, it looks remarkably good. As do you."

"Sally, you gave it to me. Remember when you took all our savings but left me this establishment to run?"

"But the B and B is worth much more than what I took. If you'd like, you can buy me out—at current market value, of course."

"I'm having none of this," Caldwell declared with more than a hint of anger. "You abandoned me, ran out with no explanation, left me to handle everything: all the bills, all the guests, all the particulars. Now you show up and think you own something? Well, I think not."

Sally leaned forward and said, "But, Caldwell, my name is still on the deed. I have checked with my lawyer, and everything is in order. How did you think you were going to sell it without me?"

He folded his arms over his chest and said, "Don't worry. I had a plan to take care of that."

Sally smiled. "I'm sure you did. But now it will be even easier with me here. You see, we can all work together. I need the money. And you need me. We can help each other."

Caldwell turned and looked at me. "No, that's not the way it's going to work. I have been planning on using the money from the sale to start our new business. You said when you left that the business was mine. A verbal agreement. Right, Karen?"

I nodded, honestly not knowing what to think. Sally sounded awfully sure of herself. But I knew that Caldwell needed me to back him up at this moment. "Caldwell's absolutely right," I said.

"Sally, your coming back trying to claim this place is horrible. After how you've treated Caldwell," said Penelope.

Alfredo lifted up his empty glass, seemingly oblivious to the tension in the air, and said, "I think it's time for another drink."

FOUR

Comfort Food

After having another drink, Sally and Alfredo carried their bags into their room and then went out for dinner. Penelope sat with us for a while, but offered little comfort. Caldwell was very quiet.

Finally he said, "Sally looks good."

I had nothing to say about her looks.

"She always looks good, especially when she's behaving badly," Penelope said with her hands wrapped over her chest. "The worse she behaves, the better she looks. It's like she sucks energy from the people she hurts."

"So you knew she might be coming?" Caldwell asked.

"I got a note from her asking me to meet her in London for dinner. Who knows why? Some whim. A little family get-together. We only have each other now that Daddy is gone and Mum is slipping away. But Sally's never been very chummy, as you know."

"Did you know she was going to stay here?" he asked.

"I didn't think she would. I still can't believe she'd have the audacity to stay here after what she did to you, but then why do I keep letting her surprise me?"

"I'm sure she wanted it to be a surprise—for all of us. That's why she used her friend's name to make the reservation. It's been quite a shock."

"You mustn't let her have her way with you," Penelope said.

Some small noise came out of my throat, rather like a yelp, as I nodded my head in agreement.

Caldwell shook his head. "Don't worry. I'll stand my ground. She's not going to walk all over me this time."

"Well, I'm exhausted." Penelope stood up. "Just breathing air in the same room as my darling sister makes me feel fatigued. And a little sick. I'm off to bed. See you in the morning."

I still wasn't clear what Penelope was even doing here. She said she had come to see her sister, but she hadn't known where Sally was staying. And they didn't seem on good terms. It all seemed very odd to me, but families are like that. Penelope went back up to her room.

Bruce the book collector came in looking very pleased with himself. He was a tall, awkward man, with thinning hair that he managed to pull back in a slight ponytail. He always wore some kind of suit coat and had pieces of paper sticking out of all the pockets. He carried a satchel that was bulging with books.

"What ho," he said.

"Evening," Caldwell answered.

I felt like saying "Tallyho!" but resisted.

"Have you had a good day?" Caldwell kindly asked, since it was so clear that Bruce was brimming over with glee.

"Yes, indeed. I found a decent copy of *The Velveteen Rabbit*. I would say it's in very good condition, maybe ever so slightly shelf-cocked. If I'm right it's worth nearly five thousand pounds."

Shelf-cocked, I knew from Caldwell, was when a book was slightly askew from sitting crooked on a shelf. I quickly translated the pounds into dollars: close to eight thousand dollars. "What a score," I said.

Bruce looked at me blankly.

Caldwell said, "Way to go, mate. May I ask what you paid?"

Bruce was squirming to tell. "I got it for half that."

"Very good," Caldwell said.

"I'll bid you two good night." Bruce went up to his room, I assumed, to organize his finds, leaving Caldwell and me alone.

"That's a lot of money," I murmured.

"Yes, but only if it's in 'very good' condition. If not, then the book is not worth much more than he paid."

"Who determines the condition?"

"We all do, but there are strict standards."

"Yes," I said. "And I suppose I'll become more familiar with them as I help you collect."

Caldwell smiled. "I'm sure you'll be excellent at categorizing a book."

"Thanks."

"I'm sorry about all this Sally stuff," he said, waving his hand.

"Now, don't worry about it," I jumped in.

"I can't help it. Sally almost always gets what she wants," he said, his voice shaking with anger. "Well, this is one time she won't."

"How will you stop her?" I asked.

"We will stop her," he said, reaching over to take my hand.

"Her name is still on the deed?" I asked reluctantly.

"Yes, I'm afraid so. But she took a substantial amount of cash when she left. She might think she's owed more money, but we'll figure out how much she owes me for running the place for almost seven years. That, along with the money she took, should be just about equal to the amount she's claiming."

I was glad to see Caldwell taking charge. "Of course, that should work."

He hugged me, then said, "What would I do without you?"

"I hate to think."

We kissed a light, conspiratorial kiss. When we pulled apart, I confessed, "I'm hungry."

"I'm not surprised. It's way past your dinnertime. How does beans on toast sound?" he asked.

We all have our own versions of comfort food. Mine is tuna casserole made exactly the way my mother had always made it: canned tuna, Campbell's cream of mushroom soup, and thick egg noodles with Parmesan cheese on top. Unfortunately, Caldwell's is a "tin" of baked beans on toasted white bread. I'm sure it offers a full complement of protein and carbohydrates, but to me it seems like starch on starch—a bit gloppy. But I knew it would make him feel better. Popeye had spinach; my darling grew strong on baked beans.

"Just what I was hoping you'd say," I answered.

"I know you're coddling me."

"Oh, I thought that was in the job description: coddle when needed."

"So you will take the job?" he asked.

"Of coddler?" I asked.

He threw the ball right back in my lap. "Karen, what would you like your job to be?"

"At the moment, friend and partner," I said, determined not to take the first step toward something more.

"That will do for this moment."

We kissed again and moved into the kitchen to make our meal.

"Let's forget about Sally for right now," I said.

"Yes, tomorrow is time enough to think about that," Caldwell agreed as he opened a can of baked beans.

A voice came from the doorway. "Forget about who?"

Brenda had some shopping in a mesh bag over her shoulder. She was in her late twenties, not a particularly attractive girl, but fresh and young. She wore her long brown hair pulled back tight into a ponytail and had on a small T-shirt that read QUEEN BEE.

"Did I hear you mention Sally?" Brenda asked.

"Yes, she's come for a visit," Caldwell said without any enthusiasm.

"Oh, how lovely. It's been so long. I wonder if she'll even remember me. I was just out of school when she left." Brenda patted her ponytail. "I had short hair then. She persuaded me to grow it long. And she taught me how to put on nail polish and eye makeup."

"Yes, I remember. I don't think she'll be staying with us for long, I'm afraid," Caldwell stated.

I was hopeful.

"I'll just pop up and say hi," Brenda said.

"She and her boyfriend have gone to dinner," Caldwell told her.

"Maybe later. This is great." Brenda deposited the breakfast supplies on the counter and ran off to her room.

"Someone's glad to see her," I said.

"Sally was good with Brenda. She took her under her wing. But then she left her without a word too. I think Brenda suffered almost as much as I did."

FIVE

Bedmates

Later, climbing into bed, I could tell Caldwell hadn't let go of the Sally problem. I somewhat reluctantly slipped off the new white satin robe he had given me as a welcome gift and hung it on the bedpost. I felt beautiful when I wore it.

Some of our sweetest moments together were tucked under the comfort of our large duvet, books in front of our faces, arms touching, pages turning, a lovely sort of harmony between us.

But tonight, the pages weren't turning very fast next to me and, when I looked at Caldwell, his face was contorted into a deep-thinking frown. He was obviously not even reading his book.

I reached over and smoothed out his forehead. "Calm yourself."

He let his book fall onto his chest and spit out, "Blast it, Karen, I can't. Just when everything was going so well, Sally has to come along and ruin it all. I had so hoped you would never have the pleasure of meeting her, and now here she is staying with us."

"You could turn her out on the street," I suggested sweetly.

"Don't think I haven't thought of that. Would they take the hint if their bags were left on the front steps and the door was locked?"

"They might, but I wouldn't put it past that woman to be able to jimmy the lock." We lay quietly for a moment, then I asked, "What had you been planning to do about her name being on the deed?"

"I guess I was trying not to think about it. But it's close to seven years now since she left. I had thought of declaring her dead."

I woke up twice that night. The first time when Sally and Alfredo stumbled up the stairs on the way to their room. They were loud and sounded drunk. Alfredo was murmuring in Italian to her, and his words sounded amorous. I was rather glad I didn't know Italian. Caldwell didn't wake, and I was glad of that too.

The second time was when a loud crash happened in the house, like the sound of huge hailstones pelting the roof, but closer. I sat up in bed and saw with concern that Caldwell was not next to me.

Fearing something awful had happened to him, I sprang up and ran out of our bedroom. Caldwell was standing down the hallway, staring into the book room, with the most horrible and disbelieving look on his face.

I wasn't sure I wanted to see what he was looking at. I walked slowly toward him as Penelope's door banged open.

"What was that noise?" she asked.

Caldwell didn't answer, but kept staring.

I came up next to Caldwell and looked in the room. I felt some relief as I saw that all that had happened was one of the bookcases had toppled over. He must have been feeling terribly worried about the condition of the books that had fallen and were tossed all over the floor.

But then I noticed he was staring at something else, and my eyes followed his down to the edge of the tidal wave of books.

What I saw was a hand, a hand reaching out from under the sea of books.

A woman's hand, red nail polish on the long, slender fingers, still as stone.

SIX

Buried by Books

The three of us scrambled to dig Sally out, even though I had a deep sense that she was not with us any longer. I feared that the fall and tsunami of books had done her in.

After we pulled up the bookcase, we carefully lifted the many heavy volumes off Sally. When we had freed the top half of her body, Caldwell had the presence of mind to send Penelope to call for help.

I knelt down next to Sally to see if I could detect any signs of life. Her head was turned to the side, and her eyes were closed. When I reached out and touched her face, it felt unresponsive.

First I checked her carotid artery, as I knew to do from taking CPR classes, which were required of all librarians. I could find no pulse. When I opened her eyes, there was no movement. But I knew that it might not be too late to save her, and so I administered CPR—putting both my hands on her chest and pumping rapidly up and down.

After many minutes of my getting no response, Penelope took over.

I stood next to Caldwell and shook my head. "I'm afraid it's no use. I think we've lost her."

"What?" he asked, seeming dazed.

"I don't think she's alive anymore," I said, just to be clear. "I'm sorry." He wrapped his arms around me.

Even though Sally was minimally dressed, in a filmy white nightgown, she seemed remarkably unmarked by the onslaught of books—which made it hard to believe she could be dead.

As I watched Penelope work on her, I noticed a trickle of blood coming from the back of Sally's head. She must have fallen over backward and hit her head with tremendous force. I supposed such a blow could kill instantaneously.

Caldwell stared at her and whispered to me, "I don't understand how this could happen. She always hated books. Do you think she knew somehow that this would be her fate?"

"If she hated books so much, what was she doing in here?" I asked, pointing to the mess around us.

Just then Bruce appeared in the doorway of the library in a rumpled bathrobe. "Here, here. What's going on?"

I said, "There's been an accident." The British habit of understatement was catching on with me.

He glanced down at Sally's body, said, "Dreadful," but then quickly began to peruse the books.

A moment later a scream came from behind us, and we all jumped.

Brenda stood in the doorway, wearing flannel pajamas with poodles all over them and her long hair streaming around her face. "Not Sally!" she cried out the name. "Not her!"

She threw herself down on the floor, grabbed one of the well-manicured hands, and held on tight, as if she could pull the woman back from the dead. Her hair tumbled over her face as she leaned forward and cried.

I put a hand on her shoulder and after a few moments lifted her up to her feet. She didn't resist but turned in to my arms and kept crying.

"I didn't even get to say hello," Brenda mumbled into my shoulder.

"I'm so sorry," I said.

Then Brenda stepped away from me. "You didn't even know her. She was a wonderful person. Better than you."

And then Alfredo stumbled through the library doorway. His hair stuck up like the crest on a woodpecker, and his eyes were as red as the bird's crest.

"What has happened to my darling?" he asked, rubbing his eyes as if he could change what he was seeing.

"I'm afraid it's not good news," I told him.

"She is just sleeping, yes?" he asked with a catch in his voice that revealed he knew this was not the case.

"A long sleep," Caldwell said.

When the paramedics arrived, two young men took over. I told them what I had done and they asked us to step out of the room, but we stayed in the doorway, watching how they would handle it.

Both of them were in very good physical shape, and somehow this reassured me—like if anyone could bring her back to life, they could. They took out the paddles and tried to shock her back, but the lifeless body made no response. They gave her a shot of what I guessed was adrenaline. No movement.

Finally they both stood up, and one of them called the time. Four eighteen in the morning.

I heard a sniffle and turned around to see Penelope crying. Her sister had just died, even if they weren't on the best of terms.

Alfredo was clearing his throat and wiping his eyes. Brenda ran down the stairs, weeping.

I looked over at Caldwell, and he was just staring at the floor, no expression at all on his face.

I reached out and took his hand. He squeezed mine, but didn't look at me. I wondered how he felt right now. I remembered how I felt when my ex-boyfriend died, like someone had cut a small chunk of flesh out of my body. Quite small but still painful. You can't be close to someone for that amount of time and not feel pain at their demise. Their death takes away a time in your life.

"What happened here?" the tall paramedic asked.

We all waited for Caldwell to answer.

He cleared his throat and said, "I would say that it appears the bookcase fell over on top of her."

"In the middle of the night?"

"Yes."

"What was she doing in here?"

Caldwell shook his head. "I have no idea. I usually keep the door locked. And Sally . . . I barely know her anymore."

"Was anyone with her? Did anyone see it happen?"

We all shook our heads and looked at Alfredo.

Alfredo said, "I was too much sleeping. We had been drinking. I did not know she had gone."

"Who's closest of kin?" the paramedic asked.

Alfredo raised his hand. "I was her fiancé. But I don't know what is this closest of kin."

Then Penelope stepped forward, giving Alfredo a sharp look. "I believe I'm actually her closest of kin. I'm her sister. What do I need to do?"

"Well, nothing at the moment. Under the circumstances, we will be calling in the police, and they will tell you what will happen."

"The police?" Penelope asked.

Caldwell added, "But surely this is an accident."

"This looks like an accidental death, but that's not for us to determine."

"Calling in the police seems too much," Penelope said.

The young, burly paramedic looked down at the lovely woman in a nearly see-through negligee. "Maybe so, but that's the next step. To determine the cause of death. It's procedure."

SEVEN

Watching the Detectives

The library turned into a crime scene. We were all asked to go downstairs and wait for the detectives to come.

Penelope flopped onto the couch and curled into a ball. Alfredo sat on the other end of the couch, leaned back, and closed his eyes. Brenda had gone to her room, and we could hear her still crying behind the door. Bruce sat in a chair next to a bookcase and started examining the books.

That left Caldwell and me to worry and stew.

"You have no idea why Sally was in the library?" I asked him.

"None whatsoever. I don't know why the door was even

open. You know I usually keep it locked. There are some very expensive books in there."

I gave a short gasp as I thought back to the afternoon. "I think it was my fault. I was working on cataloging and arranging the books when Sally arrived and, I guess, in all the excitement, I forgot to go back and lock the room. But even if I had, she probably knows where you keep the keys."

He nodded. "Yes, right where they've always been. Never occurred to me to change them."

I asked him a question that had been bothering me since I knew what he had planned to do to get her name off the deed for the house. "Did you really think Sally might have been dead?" When I saw his confused look, I added, "I mean, before tonight."

He dropped his head into his hands. "I had no idea. I hadn't heard a word from her in a few years, and that was just a postcard. I guess I thought it was possible, plus, I figured the house was mine, since she had made it so clear she no longer wanted it. I never thought she would come back and claim it. The furthest thing from my mind was Sally."

We said no more as the police arrived. After going upstairs and looking at the scene, a short, round rock of a man came in and introduced himself as Chief Inspector Blunderstone.

I had trouble not laughing at his name. He didn't look like a man who would find anything funny. And we were not in a funny situation. But still the laugh bubbled inside of me like a faucet that wouldn't turn off. I wondered if I was slightly hysterical and took some deep breaths.

Both Penelope and Alfredo stirred when he came in the room. Blunderstone walked heavy on the floor. Penelope leaned forward and wiped her face with her hands; Alfredo shook his head as if he were trying to wake up and rid himself of a horrible nightmare.

I had a sudden premonition things were going to get even worse when the first question Blunderstone asked was "Who found the body?"

Caldwell confessed, "I did."

Blunderstone took a couple of steps closer to Caldwell but kept standing. "And what is your relationship with the deceased?" was the next question.

"She was my former partner in the B and B, but she left over six years ago. I've hardly seen or heard from her since."

"When did she come back?" Blunderstone continued.

Caldwell was silent for a few moments.

"Just yesterday," I answered for him, even though I knew I should keep my mouth shut. Sometimes it's hard when you know the answer.

Alfredo jumped in and said, "She want her house back. We are going to marry, and we will live here."

Blunderstone looked at Caldwell, who nodded.

"Whose house is this?" the inspector asked.

When Caldwell still didn't say anything, I answered for him again. "It belongs to Caldwell. He's been running the B and B solo since she left."

Blunderstone swung around to face me. I noticed that he couldn't move his neck easily, so he had to turn his whole body. "And who, may I ask, are you?"

This question kept coming up. Who exactly was I? I felt like the longer I was in England, the less sure I was of how I fit into this picture. "I'm a good friend of Caldwell's."

"How good?" Blunderstone persisted.

"Good enough," I answered.

"And who are you two?" Blunderstone swung his body around to face the couch, where Penelope and Alfredo were sitting next to each other.

Penelope pulled back her hair and flung it over her shoulder. "I'm her sister and her closest of kin."

"I am her fiancé," Alfredo said.

"I assume you were sharing a room," Blunderstone put to Alfredo.

"But of course."

"And do you know why she was up in the middle of the night?" Blunderstone asked him.

"I do not know. I was sleeping."

The inspector turned back to Caldwell. "Who else is staying with you?"

"There's Brenda and Bruce. Brenda is my help. She went back to her room. And Bruce, who's over there, is a guest."

"I will need to speak with them."

"Certainly." Caldwell got up as if to go get Brenda, but Blunderstone waved him back down.

"What I would like to know . . ." the inspector humphed. "How does a bookcase fall down like that?" he asked the room.

Caldwell spoke up. "That case shouldn't have come down. Because the bookcases were so tall and the floor was so uneven, I had fastened each of them to the wall with a hook."

Blunderstone nodded, and again his whole body moved down as he moved his head. "I saw the hook, but obviously it was no longer hooked. I don't like what this is saying to me." He raised his bushy eyebrows. "Mr. Perkins, if you would please come upstairs with me so we may discuss this further."

I had a hard time not standing up and going with them to protect Caldwell. He seemed so undone, as if the stuffing had come out of him.

Just as they were leaving the room, Alfredo spoke up and pointed at Caldwell. "He did not want my Sarah to be back. He was going to sell the house without her knowing. He wished her dead . . . and now she is."

EIGHT

Tiptoeing Through the Tomes

Somehow, after our hour-of-the-wolf awakening, we made it through the morning. While I had a sense that the inspector wanted to blame someone for this horrible death, he was biding his time. Photographs were taken of the scene, cops tromped up and down the stairs, one even came in and took all our fingerprints.

Four of us sat in the garden room and ate and read and watched it rain outside. For to make the setting perfect, a slow, cruel drizzle had started—the sky a dreary slate gray, the precipitation steady and relentless.

When we were finally allowed upstairs, only Bruce went

45

to change. The rest of us remained in our nightwear. At least Penelope and I had grabbed bathrobes; hers was flannel and had teddy bears on it, mine was my new white satin robe. Caldwell was in his pin-striped cotton pajamas, and Alfredo was wearing a T-shirt and silk pajama bottoms.

Caldwell turned up the heat to accommodate us all and made us a meal of eggs, bacon, and toast. Penelope barely touched her food, and so Alfredo cleaned her plate as well as his own.

Shortly after that, Bruce strolled into the garden room, looking well rested and well dressed. He was wearing a light linen shirt with a seersucker sports coat over it and jeans, nicely straddling the line between dressy and casual.

"Is it possible to still get breakfast? I have a busy schedule today," Bruce said in a chipper voice.

I could clearly see how little Sally's death had affected him. I envied him. He could just go about his day as if nothing had happened. I felt like my life had been blown apart. To see, once again, how random life is—you get up in the night to find a book to read and you die. How was this possible?

Finally Caldwell spoke. "Yes, coffee's ready. What else would you like for breakfast?"

"Just a couple pieces of toast. I don't suppose you have any marmalade?" Bruce asked.

We sat and watched Bruce devour his meal, but when he

tried to leave for the day, Caldwell restrained him, saying the police would want to talk to all of us. No one was to leave.

Just after noon, Inspector Blunderstone came into the garden room and announced they were done for the day. He issued us orders: "Don't go into that room. Don't touch anything or move anything until I give you the go-ahead. And I would like all of you to remain here in London for the next few days."

"Do you think it was an accident?" Penelope asked.

"She was hit full force by the wall of books and fell straight backwards. Her arms were down at her sides, not up as if she had been reaching for a book up high. All of this raises many questions," he said, and gave each of us a glare.

This news hit me like a ton of books. If she had been killed, it would have been by one of us sitting in this room. Well, not me, that was all I could be sure of. And, after only a moment's thought, not Caldwell. He just didn't have a mean or violent bone in his body. Plus, his reaction to Sally's death was not that of a murderer—he seemed truly upset and sorry.

Yet I knew if the police were looking to pin Sally's death on someone, he would be their first choice. It was his house, his bookcase, his books. And he certainly had the best motive of us all. Sally had come back demanding her fair share of the B and B, whether she deserved it or not.

That left Alfredo and Penelope and Brenda, maybe even

Bruce, as long as one was suspecting. However, Bruce had no connection to Sally. With her obvious affection for Sally, I found it hard to believe it could be Brenda either.

So it was down to Penelope and Alfredo—both relatives in a sense, and that was usually who killed people, their relatives.

If it turned out Sally's death had been foul play, my prime suspect would have to be Penelope. There was obviously some bad blood between her and her sister—but how could it be so bad that she would think to kill her? What would Penelope have to gain by Sally's death?

Still, it wouldn't do to overlook Alfredo. What did we know about him and his relationship to Sally? Maybe they hadn't been as in love as he'd like us to believe. Had she written him into her will, or was she waiting for their marriage to take care of that? Again the question—what did he have to gain by her death?

∾

NINE

Too Big?

Caldwell and I had to go out that late afternoon as we had set up an appointment to see a space that we might rent for the bookshop. We both felt strange leaving the house, but the library room had been locked by the police and Alfredo and Penelope had gone into their rooms to nap and Bruce had gone out to peruse more bookshops. Brenda hadn't come out of her room since the coroner had taken the body away. We had told everyone we wouldn't be long, but it still felt unnerving to be leaving the B and B unguarded.

We climbed into Caldwell's smart car and he started the vehicle, but we sat there for a moment; then he turned to me and said, "I would never have done anything to hurt Sally."

"I know that," I assured him.

"I was mad at her, once upon a time, but not now, not anymore. After meeting you, I saw more clearly than ever that she was never right for me."

I was so happy to hear this. I thought I knew it, but having something said out loud really solidified it. "Thanks."

"Thank you for being so steadfastly by my side."

"It's where I want to be," I told him.

"Well, here we go," he said, and we set off in the small car to go to the book mecca of London—Charing Cross Road.

The space we were going to look at had been an antiques store, but the owner had died a few months ago and Caldwell had heard through the grapevine of his bookish friends that it was up for grabs. It was only a block away from Any Amount of Books, a wonderful used bookshop, and both of us felt this was to the good. People looking for books don't usually stop at only one bookshop but would easily walk over and see what we might have to offer. We would be able to ride on the coattails of this well-established shop.

Luckily we found a place to park a few blocks away, and the rain had quit as we walked the dampish streets. I breathed in deeply and wondered how many times I would stroll to what might become our new shop. The lease was pricey, but between the two of us we had the money—if Caldwell could sell the B and B, if all the proceeds were his, and if we found a cheap place to live together.

An old man met us at the front door. He introduced himself as Darcy Dickens. I had never met a real Darcy before— only knew of the one in *Pride and Prejudice*. There was a hint of the lord of the manor about this man, but he was well past the marriageable age.

"Top-notch, this place is," he said as he opened the heavy wooden door and waved us in. "Can't find a better spot for a shop than this."

When we walked into the space, the first thing that hit me was how enormous it felt, with its high, vaulted ceilings and rumpled brick floor. The second thing was how cold it felt, since it had been empty for a while. And the third thing was the smell, which was, as close as I can describe, a combination of moldy shoes and wet dog, with a hint of urine. Not a pleasant bouquet.

But when I glanced over at Caldwell, I could see he was sold. The building was long and narrow, and as we walked down the floor, I could tell he was imagining it filled with bookcases.

"It's twenty meters long," he said.

After quickly calculating that was about sixty feet, I was impressed and had to hold my tongue not to mention that it looked to be about twenty feet wide. Twelve hundred square feet could hold a lot of books—I was sure more than we had together. It was about ten times the size of his library. How in heaven's name would we fill such a huge amount of space?

"The location couldn't be better," he said.

I nodded.

"He's right about that," Mr. Dickens said. "All the swells shop here."

There wasn't much light in the space, with windows only at the front and a small one at the back.

"With some lighting," Caldwell said, "I think it will be very cozy."

I walked to the back and ran my finger down the dirty windowpane. A good scrub would clean that right up.

"What do you think?" he asked.

I didn't want to explode his balloon, which was what I thought I would do if I said anything halfway realistic. "It's not bad," I said.

"Is this American understatement?"

"I do like where it is," I said truthfully.

"Can't you just see it with floor-to-ceiling bookcases, a counter by the front door, three or four easy chairs scattered about for easy reading? I actually think I might need to buy more books to fill the space."

And now I did say the truth. "I have a hard time visualizing. I'm rather a literal person. Feet on the ground."

"And that's a good place for them to be," Mr. Dickens told me as he stamped his on the floor.

"Yes," Caldwell said as he put his arm around my waist. "And you will keep me grounded too, won't you?"

I envisioned Caldwell and his balloon sailing up into the sky with me dragging him down by his feet. I wasn't sure that was the role I wanted to play in his life. I liked it that he had such lovely dreams. "Not always," I said.

"We don't have to decide today," Caldwell assured me.

"Yes, take your time. I haven't shown it to another soul, and it won't be advertised for another week," Mr. Dickens said.

I didn't really think a week was time enough to make such a big decision. "What kind of lease would you want?"

"The usual. A five-year lease."

I smiled while I quickly did some calculations and came up with an astronomical figure that made my heart sink. "Yes, well, we need to talk about this. It's a big decision."

Mr. Dickens turned from me and looked at Caldwell. "You won't find anything finer than what's right in front of you."

I had to agree with him when it came to Caldwell.

We said our thanks and good-byes to Mr. Dickens and then were quiet on our walk back to the car.

When I was seated in the car, I burst out, "I don't know. It seems overwhelming." I wasn't sure if I was talking about the shop or this huge change in my life.

"Yes, but this is a once-in-a-lifetime opportunity—to get a shop right here in the heart of the book world. I'm just not sure we should pass it up."

"But it's happening so fast, and it's so much money."

"If this book I've found is worth half what I think it is, we could easily put down enough for a deposit on the place."

"But, Caldwell, we don't really know what we're doing yet." I decided I wouldn't mention the demise of Sally or the possibility that the B and B would no longer be solely his.

He said, quietly, "We don't?"

"Not yet. Remember I've come on a trial run," I answered quietly. "And I think this space is too much for us. Too big and too expensive."

"Oh," he said. The pin had come out and popped his fantastic balloon. It had to happen. We had to be sensible.

TEN

A Penny for Your Thoughts

When we got back to the B and B, Brenda met us at the door. She had always reminded me of a dormouse, with her thin lips and twitchy ears. Her ears were in a major twitch at the moment.

"He found the sherry," she said as soon as we stepped inside.

"Who found what?" Caldwell asked.

And of course she repeated what she had said, even though he had heard her the first time and what he really wanted was an explanation.

"He being?" he asked.

"That Italian bloke, name like a kind of spaghetti. He drank the whole bottle and has now passed out on the love seat."

"You sure he's just passed out?" I asked, worried about any more troubles.

"Yes, I did the feather test," she said.

"What?" Caldwell asked.

I could tell he was upset by everything and had wanted to come home to a peaceful house.

Just in case he really didn't know what it was, I explained, "You stick a feather under someone's nose and if they're breathing, the feather moves."

While Brenda wasn't very fond of me and often disagreed with me, this once she acknowledged that I was right. "It moved."

She led us into the garden room, where we found Alfredo hanging over the edges of the love seat, one arm dangling to the floor, the other behind his head. A small feather was still attached to his upper lip. His mouth hung open and his cheek was squished into a pillow, making his face look longer and thinner than it already was. A handsome fellow when sober and not sleeping, he had turned into a caricature of himself.

"It got stuck, the feather," Brenda explained.

"Don't worry. He won't notice," I assured her, then turned to Caldwell and asked, "How much was left in the bottle?"

"Well, I opened it for him last night and he had two small drinks from it. So quite a lot."

"Do you think we should wake him?" I asked.

"No, it's quieter with him sleeping. He's not going to feel very good when he does wake up, so let's put it off," Caldwell said, and I could tell he just wanted to put everything off, follow Alfredo's example, and have a couple glasses of wine, I hoped not to the passing-out point.

"He was ever so upset about Miss Sally's death," Brenda said.

"Yes, he was bound to be. They were to be married," Caldwell said.

"Really? I wondered," Brenda said. "He was muttering something about a ring."

"Maybe they were planning on buying a ring here in London," Caldwell suggested.

"I don't know." Brenda grew pensive. "He made it sound like it had already been bought."

"Well, then maybe a romantic proposal?" I said.

Brenda shrugged.

"Have you heard anything more from the police?" Caldwell asked.

"No, it's been surprisingly quiet, once *he* nodded off."

"Penelope still around?" he asked.

"Yes, she's been in her room since you left."

Caldwell looked at me. "Let's just eat here tonight. Something simple."

"Fine," I said. "As long as it isn't beans on toast."

"How about pasta with marinara sauce?"

"That sounds scrumptious." I leaned in and kissed him on the nose. He just looked like he needed a light kiss. Behind us Brenda cleared her throat in an unhappy sort of way.

"Brenda, would you care to join us?" he asked.

"No, I'm off to see my mum. I'll probably stay overnight there. She's been poorly of late."

"I'm going to change into something more comfortable," I said, and went up the stairs, not looking forward to seeing the off-limits library.

When I got to the top of the stairs, I saw the tape was still strung across the entrance to the library, but the door was open a crack. I walked quietly to the door and peeked in. Penelope was standing on her tiptoes, scanning the books.

I wondered what she was looking for, but I really wondered why she thought the message on the tape didn't apply to her. It very clearly stated: CRIME SCENE—DO NOT ENTER.

"Penelope," I said in a quiet but carrying tone.

Still she jumped and shrieked and put a hand on her heart. "Oh, you scared me. These books make me so nervous. I can't help thinking of Sally and what they did to her."

I held up the tape so she would get the hint to leave the room. She caught on and walked toward me, then ducked under the tape.

"How did you get in?" I asked.

"I knew where the keys were from before . . . when I was here before." She looked and sounded rattled.

"What were you doing in there if it's making you so nervous?" I asked. I decided not to point out that she wasn't supposed to be in the room. This might be a good chance to talk to her alone, and I wanted to take advantage of it.

"I, well, I was just curious, you know."

"About what?"

"Why Sally was in here last night."

"Yes, that's a good question. Do you have any ideas?"

Penelope nodded her head and then said slowly, "Maybe she was looking for something."

"A book?"

"Maybe."

"But she had such a reputation as a nonreader."

"She read all sorts of things, just not anything that Caldwell would approve of," Penelope said.

"Like what?"

"Oh, you know, magazines and gossipy stories. She loved to follow the royalty and the movie stars."

I couldn't help wondering what Caldwell had seen in Sally. The more I learned about her, the more their relationship seemed odd. What could it have been based on? I hated to think it was just sex, but maybe it was.

"What did she and Caldwell have in common?" I asked, not really expecting an answer.

But Penelope spoke up immediately. "They both liked to cook. Sally liked to garden, and Caldwell liked that. Sally could be very charming when she put her mind to it." Penelope paused for a moment and sighed. "Unfortunately, she didn't care for his love of books as much. She felt like his books just got in the way."

"Why did she leave him?" I asked, since Penelope seemed to have more information than I would have given her credit for.

"She gets tired of things very easily. She's been like that since we were kids. I think the bed-and-breakfast was her idea, but then she didn't like how much work it was. She said that no one should have to talk to people before they've had their caffeine in the morning. She saw herself as the grande dame of the manor, but turned out the job she had made her feel more like the maid. Plus, she never liked to be tied down."

"Did you know she was going to leave him?"

"No, Sally and I weren't close like that. She did send me postcards from Chicago and then Italy. I visited her in the small village where she was living—outside of Rome. The air was soft and the light was more golden than here. I could understand why she liked it there. And she seemed to fit in. Alfredo was wonderful to me. He even taught me some Italian. What a beautiful language."

"You said you knew she was coming back to London?"

"Yes, she had written me a note saying she was coming with Alfredo, but I didn't know why."

"You didn't know she was going to claim the house back?"

"No, I'm really surprised. She always seemed so happy to be away from here. She loved Italy."

"But it sounds like all she wanted was the money. Did she and Alfredo have money problems?"

Penelope hesitated before saying, "I'm not sure. Alfredo lived in an old villa, very grand, but rather falling down. I would imagine it would take a lot of money to keep it up."

"What does he do for a living?" I wondered.

"He opens up his house a couple of days a week for tourists to come and see it. I guess you could say that he's a tour guide. That's how he and Sally met. She came to visit his villa and never left."

"Is there any reason you can imagine anyone wanting to hurt Sally—if that's what happened here?" I asked. A simple question, but one that stalled out on Penelope.

She looked at the floor, then the ceiling, then sighed. "I only know what you know."

But I knew Penelope wasn't telling me everything.

ELEVEN

Cooking the Books

"So Sally was a good cook?" I asked as I wrapped the last few noodles of spaghetti around my fork, careful not to flick any of the sauce on my blouse.

Caldwell stared off into space. He wasn't eating much, which was unusual. He had stirred his spaghetti into a sort of bird's nest. "Yes, now that I think about it, she was a good cook. Never followed recipes, which drove me crazy. She would look at them and then start to improvise. Sometimes the dishes turned out very well; other times, not so good."

"Are you feeling sad?" The question popped out of me. I know men don't like such questions, but I hoped that Caldwell was different.

He looked over at me; his big brown eyes softened into mine. "No. Not really. I just feel like someone turned me upside down and shook me. Here we were planning to figure out how to start our life together. I was looking forward to spending long days with you, going to bookshops, reading, organizing the books I've collected. And then Sally decided to burst back into my life and take back the B and B. And just as she's upset everything, she dies."

"Oh," I said. An encouraging "oh" I hoped.

He looked down at the mess he had made of his plate. "Sally has always managed to mess things up. She could never just let things be. To tell you the truth, what I'm really feeling is scared."

I pushed his plate aside and took his hand. "But you're not alone."

He smiled, but it was a weak production. "I know, but I think that's making it worse. I feel bad that you're mixed up in this."

"Mixed up in what? I'm glad I'm here to give you support. And this will all be over soon. Alfredo and Penelope will be gone in a few days, and we can get back to thinking about the bookshop."

He shook his head. "I know, but the police don't seem

to be treating her death like it was an accident. I'm not so worried about myself, but I'd hate to see anything happen to you."

I squeezed his hand tight, all the while wondering why he was worrying about me. I hadn't done anything to Sally. Did he think I had?

Alfredo stuck his head into the kitchen, where we were eating. "That has a very good smell," he said. His dark hair was sticking up in back, once again giving him the look of a woodpecker. But he seemed revived by his nap.

Caldwell got a clean plate down from the cupboard and put on it the leftovers from the serving dish. *"Buon appetito."*

"Grazie," Alfredo said and sat down in Caldwell's chair. He seemed more than able to make himself at home no matter where he was or what was going on. I envied his ability to ask for what he wanted. More to the point, to know what he wanted, even if it was only food and drink.

Unlike Caldwell, Alfredo ate with great gusto, sipping the noodles down his throat. *"Molto bene."* He put his hands on either side of Caldwell's face and, for a moment, I thought he was going to kiss him, but he just gave him a friendly shaking. "As good as my mama's."

High praise indeed.

"Alfredo, did you know that Sally was coming back to London to reclaim this B and B?"

"To reclaim?" he asked.

"Yes, to demand a part of this house." I waved my hands, trying to encompass the whole house.

"Oh, *sì*. We talk and she tell me that we can have some money from this house. We need it for my villa, you know. But I did not know that she kept this a secret from you, Caldwell."

"You thought I knew she was coming?" Caldwell asked.

"Yes, she tell me we will be most welcome. I'm sorry that you did not know the truth about the visit." He stopped eating, and his fork was held up in the air like he was hoping the noodles would take flight. "I am very sad about my Sally. How can she be gone like this? It is too much to believe." Tears started running down his face as if someone had turned on a faucet in his eyes. This was certainly a man who had no trouble showing his emotions.

Caldwell looked at me with *help* written in his eyes. I gently touched Alfredo's noodle-holding hand, then patted it. He pushed his plate back, rested his head in his hands on the table, and wept great, gasping sobs.

Caldwell carried our two plates to the sink. I knew he wanted to leave Alfredo to me.

When Alfredo lifted up his head, I handed him a napkin, which he took and immediately blew his nose in. "Thank you so much," he said, and wiped his eyes. "I cannot believe any of this. How could this have happened? Sally was not one to die easily."

"Do you have any idea what she was doing in the library room at night?"

"I might think that she was sleepwalking. She did that from time to time. But no, I think she was looking for something."

"What would she be looking for in the books?"

"I think she left something here that she wanted to come back for, something special to her. I don't know, but that is what I feel."

"Could it have been a book?" Caldwell asked.

"No, that is not what I think. Something small, but no book. Something more special than that."

"There's really only books in that room," I said under my breath, thinking, *And what is more special than a book?*

"We begin to talk about getting married, you know. Sally, she likes to be engaged. More official. But we don't talk about a wedding yet. I think she is not sure I am a good man for marriage."

This statement really surprised me. "How do you mean?"

"Well, yes, there is the villa, but Sally, she call it the villa palooza, saying it's more trouble than it's worth. My family home, but my family not take very good care of it." He shrugged his shoulders.

"Were you planning on living in England then?" I asked.

"No, no plans. Just come to get some money and see what happens next. That's the way Sally like to live. Day to day. But me, I miss the villa. I live there most of my life. To me it is *bella*."

When Alfredo had resumed eating and Caldwell was doing the dishes, I excused myself and went upstairs. I was going to go down to our bedroom, but I stopped as I came to the library.

There were two doors to the room. One was strung with the barrier tape. The other had once opened into a hallway right by the bathroom, but it had been blocked off from the inside when Caldwell put up a bookcase in front of it.

I walked around to examine the second door. Looking up, I could see the transom over the door with the top of the bookcase visible above it. How hard would it be for someone, a tallish someone, to push open the transom, reach in and unhook the bookcase, and push it over?

The hook had not been pulled out of the wall, so it must have been undone. It was possible that Brenda had done that when she was doing her rare dusting in the room—but why? And how could someone push that heavy bookcase over without Sally seeing them?

Which led me to the all-important question: What exactly had happened to Sally last night?

TWELVE

Skewered

The next morning we were all gathered in the garden room, having our first cups of tea or coffee, when there came a banging at the door, much louder than was necessary for us to hear it. Caldwell stood to answer it; I put down my teacup; Penelope put her hands to her mouth; Alfredo lowered the newspaper he was trying to read. Bruce didn't budge from staring at a map of the city. Brenda came in and asked if she should get the door.

Caldwell said, "No, I'll see to it," and left the room.

I picked up my teacup and tried to pretend that everything was all right, but I saw bad news in the bottom of my cup.

A moment later I heard Inspector Blunderstone's voice, unmistakable in its authority and loudness. Finally, not being able to stand it any longer, I stood, excused myself, and hustled down the hallway. Brenda followed me, I assumed on her way to the kitchen, but probably wanting to see what was going on.

"Your fingerprints were the only ones found on the bookcase," Blunderstone was saying. "How do you explain that?"

"Easy enough. After all, they would be, wouldn't they, since I'm the one who set the bookcases up and almost the only person who ever goes in there. There's really no mystery to that."

"But how do you explain the bookcase coming unhooked and tipping forward?"

"Possibly a small earthquake happened and unhooked it," Caldwell said, sounding a mite angry.

Why was he taking the bait from Blunderstone? He knew better than that. This was serious business. I wanted to shush him, but instead I stood quietly by his side and resisted reaching out to take his hand.

"Yes, well, we'll see about that." The inspector was reacting as I would have expected—quite taken aback by Caldwell's comment. "I'd like you to get your coat and come down to the station with me."

At this request, Caldwell turned and looked at me. In

this glance, I read much—a sorry-for-having-to-leave-you look, a plea to take care of things while he was gone, and also fear that he was going to be blamed for something he hadn't done. The fear was the only thing I could try to remedy.

I stepped forward and asked politely, "How long do you think you'll be detaining Mr. Perkins?"

"As long as it takes," Blunderstone barked.

"Yes, I understand, but he has a business to run, and it would be helpful to know when he might return."

At this Blunderstone really looked at me. "We won't keep him all day unless we have to. Some of my men will be staying on to search the house more thoroughly. The inquest will be held in a day or two. This will determine what the cause of death was and what more needs to happen."

"Caldwell, would you like me to call your lawyer?" I asked, not knowing if he had an official lawyer, but sure I could track one down if I needed to.

"No, Karen. It won't be necessary to call my solicitor. I have nothing to hide. This won't take long, I assure you. I'll be back in a jiff."

And then Blunderstone left, taking Caldwell with him. He seemed unconcerned about this, so I decided I would try to act the same, even if I didn't feel it.

I turned to find Brenda hovering behind me. "Well, Brenda," I said to her, "could you clean up the breakfast dishes? I think I'll go out for a walk and be back shortly. Just need to clear my head."

She gave me a dark look but nodded that she would do as I asked. I knew she was upset about Caldwell too.

When I went back into the garden room to let the others know I would be gone for a while, as would Caldwell, and that there would be officers searching the house and they might want to consider going out for a time too, I found Penelope and Alfredo sitting next to each other and talking quietly.

I told them the news.

Penelope said, "That will be fine. Alfredo and I were just discussing what to do about the funeral. I think we'll have it here in London. My mum lives just out the way in Kingsland. A small service, as Sally requested, at the funeral home."

It sounded so normal that I had a hard time connecting it with the tragedy of all that was happening to us: Caldwell taken down to the police station, a room cordoned off, and the possibility of foul play, as Inspector Blunderstone suspected.

"Of course. If there's anything we can do, let us know. I'm so sorry," I said. However, I was glad to see that Alfredo and Penelope had decided to work together on this instead of fighting over whose dead body it was. I was sure that Penelope had all rights to her sister and that she was being kind to Alfredo, which made me like her better.

Just then a group of four officers came in and asked to have the keys to all the rooms. I had them follow me to the kitchen and asked Brenda to stay and make sure they had everything they needed.

"How long will this take?" I asked of the tall officer who appeared to be in charge of the crew.

"That's rather hard to say, ma'am. But a half day's time might be a fair reckoning."

"What are you looking for?" I couldn't help asking.

"We often don't know until we find it."

I thought how true that is in many instances.

As I went up to my bedroom to make sure everything was in order, wondering if there was any incriminating evidence there. Then I shook myself. What a silly thought. They would find Kleenex and books in the bedcovers, revealing some of our bad habits; my American passport in the bureau drawer, making me an alien; and plans for the bookshop spread out on the desk.

What might the police make of that—the fact that Caldwell was planning on changing careers? Could that be seen as suspicious?

After grabbing my purse, I went downstairs, said goodbye to a scowling Brenda, and walked out the door without the slightest idea where I was going. Away. I just wanted and needed to get away. Once again a lovely trip to England was being ruined by an untimely death.

I wandered down streets, turning left, then right until I almost didn't know where I was. Most unusual for me. I always knew which direction I was facing and rarely got lost, but this was an exceptional time.

Finally I found myself in front of a shop with the most wonderful blankets and quilts in the window. A small sign said: ON OFFER. I was pretty sure that meant there was a sale going on. I felt drawn into the shop.

When I went inside I found the most delightful and comfortable interior: small velvet couches with piles of woven woolen blankets, baskets with embroidered pillows, shelves full of nicely folded quilts. I ran my hands over the closest coverlet.

"All from Wales," a tall, stork-like woman with dark hair appeared from behind a screen and told me. "Handmade, some quite old. Some more recent."

"I'm just looking," I said, having no intention of buying anything.

"We're all just looking," she intoned back to me. "I'm sorting out some things, but give a call if you need any assistance." And with that she disappeared behind the screen.

I felt like I had stumbled into someone's country estate. Truth be told, I wanted everything in the shop. But I walked toward a pile of blankets and found myself pulling out a golden striped one with just a thread of red running through it.

Wouldn't that look nice at the end of our bed? I thought. Which made me think of Caldwell, and a huge weight descended on me. I sat down on the couch next to the pile of blankets and held the golden one in my lap, petting it as if it were an animal that could comfort me.

Did Caldwell know something about Sally's death that he hadn't told me? Would he have wanted our dream of a bookshop to come true so badly that he would have done something to his ex-partner? But even as these questions rose in me, the thought of him, how dear he was, grew, and I knew there was no way he could have harmed her.

I stood up, shaking these possibilities out of my mind, causing the blanket to fall to the floor.

The stork woman must have heard me; she rounded the screen again and found me folding up the golden blanket.

"Oh," she said, "that is a most unusual and lovely piece. I found it in a small town called Rhayader, right in the middle of Wales. I would think it's over fifty years old, and in absolutely perfect condition. Yes, you've chosen a particularly nice example of Welsh woolens."

Regretfully, I set it down on top of the pile. "As I said, I'm just looking. Not in a place to buy anything," I confessed.

"Well, if you change your mind come back quickly. That blanket won't last long. Especially now that everything's on offer."

"Thank you," I said, and, with one backward glance at the golden blanket, I left the store. I had no future to count on—not knowing what I wanted, not knowing what was to happen to the B and B or to Caldwell.

It was no time to indulge in a blanket, even if it did offer the only comfort available at the moment.

THIRTEEN

Questioning Everything

I sat by myself in the late-afternoon sun that was coming in the garden room window, waiting for Caldwell to return. The remains of Sally's untended garden showed through the windows. Although the neglected flower beds made me feel bad, gardening was simply not an interest of Caldwell's, and I certainly wasn't ready to take it on.

Alfredo and Penelope had gone off to make arrangements for Sally's funeral. Brenda had left to visit her mum. Bruce had a long list of bookstores he was going to check out. I felt very much alone.

So I did what I often do when I'm feeling lonely—called

Rosie. If my timing was right, I'd catch her right before the library opened and maybe she'd have time to talk for a few minutes.

"Sunshine Valley Library," she answered.

"You have any good books on how to handle the coppers in England?"

"Oh no. Don't tell me."

"Okay, I won't."

"Shut up! Karen, what is going on?"

"Rosie, it's too terrible. Caldwell's old girlfriend, Sally, showed up at the B and B."

"No," she said.

"Yes, but that's not all. Her sister, Penelope, was here too, and Sally brought her new boyfriend."

"Oh, that's good."

"But wait. She wanted to take back her share of the B and B. And maybe even Caldwell as well."

"No way."

"But then things got even worse."

"How?" she asked.

"A bookcase fell over on top of her and killed her."

"I don't believe it."

"But it gets worse."

"How can it?"

"There is a slight chance she might have been murdered and"—my voice faltered, but I forced myself to go on—"I'm afraid they suspect Caldwell."

Silence.

"Rosie?"

"I'm not sure this move to England is a good idea at all, Karen. Even if it means I have a place to stay in London."

"What am I to do?"

"Well, obviously, you must find out if she was murdered, then find out who did it, then rescue Caldwell, which will put him forever in your debt, and then get married before somebody else dies."

"Yes, I guess that's right."

"Any more questions?"

"I wish you would come over here. I feel quite alone."

"First of all, Nancy would have a conniption fit; secondly, the library needs me; thirdly, there's Richard; and finally, I'm only a phone call away."

"Right."

"What are you going to do now?"

"Go sniff around and see if I can discover anything that will save Caldwell's neck. However, it would be surprising if I could find something the cops have missed."

"This does sound bad."

"Thanks for your help."

"Any time."

"How's Richard?"

"He thinks he loves me."

"That's wonderful."

"Yes, but I'm not ready yet."

"To say it back or to hear it said?"

"I think both."

"What have you got to lose?"

"My independence?" she asked.

I knew how she was feeling. So similar to the questions I was asking myself about coming to live with Caldwell. "What do you have to gain?"

"A great guy, a life together."

I thought of Caldwell. What was I dillydallying around for? When the police gave him back to me, I would welcome him with open arms.

"Sounds like a no-brainer to me," I told her, wondering if it really was.

"Gotta go. Call me later about the search."

When I got off the phone, I heard the front door open and rushed to see who was coming in, hoping it was Caldwell.

But it was only Bruce. However, he was loaded down with books and I stepped forward to take a bundle from his hands.

"Thanks so much," he said as he relinquished them.

"You did well today," I commented.

"Oh, yes, some lovely finds. I would say a good day's work," he said. "Would you like to see?"

"My, yes," I said, and we walked down to the garden room.

I let him have the sofa so he could spread his books on the coffee table. Maybe it was called a tea table in England. I'd have to ask Caldwell. If he ever returned. But the books Bruce was revealing took my mind off Caldwell for a moment.

"Why, they're all children's books," I noticed.

"Yes, that's my specialty."

I picked up a book I had loved as a child, *Five Children and It*. It had no slipcover but showed four children looking down at a large, blob-like snail creature. The cover was red with gilt lettering. "This is one of my favorites."

"Yes, Nesbit has had good staying power. And that's a first edition, with a signature, which of course pops the price up. I was lucky to find it. Probably my best discovery of the day."

I knew one should not ask, but I couldn't help it. "Where did you find such a book? What might it fetch in resale?"

Bruce grew quite animated as he told me, "I found the book tucked away in an antiques shop, and I don't think they quite realized what they had. It was only a couple hundred pounds."

Not cheap, I thought. I was coming to realize that this was a business for Bruce, much as he loved books, and that his main concern was making money on his finds. I hoped Caldwell and I had some of that drive.

"And I think it will probably bring in over twice that—

maybe even three times," he said happily. "Well, I'll just cart these all upstairs."

"I'm sorry to tell you the police went through your room," I said.

"Oh dear. Not good, is it? What do they think has gone on here?" he asked. "Might I talk with Caldwell?"

"I'm still sorry to say that he's not here. He hasn't returned from the police station."

Bruce picked up his latest find and held it to his chest as if someone might want to take it from him. "Are they thinking he might have had something to do with that nasty death?"

"I guess so."

Bruce gathered up all his books and left me wilting on a chair.

For a moment I let this possibility bloom, Caldwell reaching through the transom and pushing over the bookcase. But as soon as that thought came into my mind, I banished it. I would never believe Caldwell killed Sally, unless he told me so himself. And even then I would think he was covering up for someone else.

The man who couldn't kill a mouse certainly couldn't push a wall of books over on a former lover, no matter how mad he was at her.

Just then I heard the door open.

I went to the end of the hall and watched Caldwell come through the entryway. Just what I wanted to see.

I rushed into his arms.

But before I could properly attend to him, I saw that a police officer was standing behind him and looking at me.

"Ma'am, I have to ask you to come with me to the station. Inspector Blunderstone wants a few words."

FOURTEEN

Where Were You?

For some reason, even though I knew I was in modern-day London, I expected the police station to be some charming old building. Far from it, the station I entered looked like the corporate headquarters of a multinational company. While many of the people swarming the building were dressed in street clothes, the majority were wearing some type of a uniform. They all looked harried and intent.

The young officer who had escorted me took me to a small room with a small window that looked out onto a city street. He told me to sit by a table and that Inspector Blunderstone would be with me shortly.

I had not had time to look myself over before we left the B and B. I ran my hands through my hair, sure that I was only making matters worse, and wondered if I should try to apply some lipstick, but decided against it. I was going to be questioned about a death, not having a job interview.

Blunderstone walked in, holding a sheaf of papers in his hands. He sat down, put the papers into an open file folder, and gave me a nod. A young woman police officer came in behind him, shut the door, then stood up against the wall. I wondered if she was there for my protection or so, later on, I couldn't claim that Blunderstone had had his way with me. Whatever the reason, I was glad of her presence, although she did not look much friendlier than the inspector.

"How long have you known Caldwell Perkins?" he asked, still looking down at the papers in his lap.

I didn't have to think but a moment to answer that question. I could have answered it almost to the hour, but I resisted. "I met him last fall. We've known each other for nearly six months."

"How did you come to meet him?"

"I was a guest at his B and B."

"Just yourself?" He lifted his head up and squinted at me.

"Yes, my traveling companion bowed out at the last minute."

"I see," he said.

I knew he didn't. The calmness of my voice in no way

acknowledged the trauma of that event. My boyfriend had dumped me hours before we were to leave for my first trip to London. And then things had proceeded to get worse. But I didn't think now was the time to mention the other deaths.

"And you've become close with Mr. Perkins?" he asked.

"Yes, quite close," I acknowledged proudly. "We have so much in common. We both love books."

He humphed, and I took that to mean that he didn't need the gory details of our bookish romance. "What do you do, Ms. Nash, when you are not visiting our lovely city?"

"I'm a librarian."

I thought I saw a flicker of a smile cross his face. "And you're from where in the States?"

"Minnesota. Sunshine Valley, which is a suburb of Minneapolis."

"Minnesota?" He thought for a moment, thumping his lip with a forefinger, then smiled. "Jesse Ventura, the wrestling governor."

Of all the things to be known for. I forced a smile. "Yes, our former governor. I didn't vote for him, but I actually agreed with him on a few issues."

"How well did you know Ms. Burroughs?"

"Not at all. I had only just met her the afternoon before . . ." I waved my hand to encapsulate all that had happened.

"And am I to understand that she was Mr. Perkins's former partner—both business and otherwise?"

"Yes, that's right."

"And that she had come back to claim her share of the B and B?"

"Well, she said that's what she wanted. But she had left the business to Caldwell when she deserted him."

"How did she desert him?"

"From what he's told me, Sally cleaned out their bank account and left without a word. Just a note saying he could have the B and B."

"Have you seen this note?"

"No, but I believe Caldwell."

Blunderstone made a slight snorting noise through his nose. "And how did you feel about Ms. Burroughs's reappearance, reclaiming the B and B?"

Here I stopped for a moment to collect myself. I was worried and tired. I didn't want to say anything wrong. I decided to just tell the truth and not to try to figure out what Blunderstone might make of it. "I thought it was preposterous. She had been gone nearly seven years, during which time Caldwell had made a success of the business. Without any warning she descends on us and claims that he owes her half the B and B. I think not."

"Did they have any legal documents drawn up when she left?"

"Not that I'm aware of. I doubt it, since Caldwell didn't even know she was leaving him."

For the first time he made a note of something on a piece of paper sitting in his lap.

"And what exactly is your relationship with Caldwell Perkins?"

The question of the hour. "We are trying to sort that out. Caldwell would like me to move over here. We had talked of selling the B and B, then starting a bookshop together."

"So it would be in your best interest if Ms. Burroughs hadn't come back or if she would just disappear."

"I see them as two separate issues. I don't feel that Sally has much of a claim on the B and B, and, even if she did, Caldwell and I might still go ahead with our plans to start a new business."

"Did you feel threatened by her?"

I thought of how I had felt when she showed up, looking so lovely and pulled together. "I wouldn't say that. More in awe. I always envy women who are taller than I am. She was a stunning woman, very sophisticated. More I felt irritated by the wrench she was throwing into the works."

"I've been told that you were the last person to be in the library that afternoon. Is that correct?"

"Yes, as far as I know. I had started organizing Caldwell's books. I was working on them when Sally arrived."

"And Mr. Perkins told me that the door to the library is usually kept locked."

"Yes, there are many valuable books in there, first editions and whatnot. But I think I forgot to lock the door when I ran to let Sally in."

"And you never went back to the library."

"No. It was a very upsetting day—what with her wanting the B and B back and her lover showing up—and I simply forgot."

"Who knew about the library?" he asked.

"What do you mean?"

"Who knew the library was there?"

"Well, I guess just about everyone did—except Alfredo. But he might have too. Sally could have told him. The library was no secret. Caldwell just didn't want people going in there without him. He had collected many first editions worth many hundreds of pounds." I didn't feel I needed to mention the very valuable book Caldwell had just found; it could have nothing to do with this death.

"Why do you think Ms. Burroughs went into the library? Odd to do it in the middle of the night."

"I have no idea."

"Might she have been there to take one of these valuable volumes?"

"That's a possibility, but I doubt it. I don't think she knew which ones they were. She had so little interest in books."

"Caldwell wouldn't have told her when they were living together?"

"You'd have to ask him, but I doubt it. He has said that she was rather jealous of his books, all the attention he paid to them. I'd be surprised if he brought them up much at all."

"Tell me what happened that night," he said.

"Well, Sally and Alfredo went out. Caldwell and I ate in. Penelope went to her room. Caldwell and I went to bed rather early. We always read in bed together. We both fell asleep. A while later I heard Alfredo and Sally coming up the stairs. They were rather loud and sounded like they were drunk. I went back to sleep. Then there was a huge crash."

I stopped for a moment to remember and felt a wash of fear sweep over me again. "Since Caldwell wasn't in bed I was afraid something had happened to him. I ran out into the hallway and saw him standing in the open doorway of the library. Horror was on his face. You know the rest."

"When had Caldwell left your bed?"

I closed my eyes and shook my head. "That I can't tell you because I'm not sure. I didn't wake up."

"When did you first notice he was gone?"

"When I heard the loud crash."

"So he could have been gone for some time?"

"I guess."

"Do you know why he left the bed?"

"I would have assumed he went downstairs to get a glass

of juice—or even more probably, to pee. He does that some-times in the night."

"Who appeared next on the scene?"

"I think Penelope. She was right down the hall. She helped us lift the bookcase off Sally. Then Bruce came into the room, but he wasn't much help. He kept wanting to look at the books. Brenda appeared and screamed. I think all the noise we were making awakened Alfredo, because he came stumbling out of their room, looking very sleepy."

The inspector was taking notes. "And what is the rela-tionship of all these people to each other?"

I was surprised he was asking me these questions—didn't he already know the answers? But maybe he was checking what each of us said against the others. "Penelope was Sally's sister, Alfredo was her fiancé, Brenda worked for Caldwell and had known Sally quite well, and Bruce was just a guest, a book collector who had heard of Caldwell's collec-tion online."

"What about you and Mr. Perkins? Is it true that you are considering being more than business partners? Life part-ners, shall we say?"

"We haven't decided. I love my job, but we have be-come close. I was here to see how I might fit into his life in London."

"I expect then that Ms. Burroughs showing up might have put the kibosh on all your plans?"

I stayed steady. "Not necessarily. You're assuming that she would have gotten what she wanted."

"And what would you have done to prevent that?"

"Nothing untoward. We would have worked within the legal system."

"As you might have gathered, Ms. Nash, we are beginning to suspect that Ms. Burroughs's death was not accidental. It is looking more and more like someone purposefully pushed the bookcase over on top of her. I won't go into the details here, but what do you think of that?"

I started to go cold in my feet. The icy feeling moved upward. I was afraid if it reached my heart, it would just stop. I found myself forced to say, "Caldwell would never do a thing like that. He is a truly gentle man."

Blunderstone nodded and shut his folder. "But what about you, Ms. Nash? Could you have done it?"

FIFTEEN

Too Little

"I'm sure they think she's been murdered," I told Caldwell as soon as I walked in the door. He pulled me to him and held me tight. His warm hug was exactly what I needed. I could feel my breathing slow and my sense of the real world returning. I was where I was supposed to be.

"Yes, I got that feeling too when I was questioned," he said after a few moments. "We'll just have to wait for the inquest. But we have nothing to worry about as neither of us had anything to do with it."

As he said that it occurred to me that Caldwell might suspect me of having pushed over the bookcase—like the chief inspector had insinuated. I was the last one in the library, I was the one who was organizing everything, Caldwell wasn't with me when the bookcase fell.

I pulled out of his arms and said, "I didn't do it."

He gathered me back in and said, "Of course you didn't, Karen. I know that. You were sound asleep in our bed when it happened. Plus, why would you want to hurt Sally?"

"Oh, I can think of lots of reasons: jealousy, fear, anger, money, love." I counted them off on my fingers. "All the usual reasons for homicide."

He took my hands in his and tried to calm me again. "But you didn't. You're my logical librarian. You work things out with your intellect, not by taking action and doing violence."

He was right. The thought of pushing a bookcase over on someone, even someone I didn't particularly care for, did make me feel revulsion.

"If the police are looking seriously at either one of us, it's me," Caldwell continued. "The scorned former lover, not wanting her to have any part of the B and B, possibly even hiding some deep, dark secret she held over my head."

"A secret?" I asked.

"I'm just surmising."

"Where had you gone that night?" I felt it was time I asked that question as long as we were clearing the air.

"Oh, my stomach was feeling quite queasy from all the

stress of the day, so I went down to have some bicarbonate of soda water to settle it. I was in the kitchen when I heard the bookcase fall."

"I'm sorry for even asking you that."

"No, don't be. We need to be truthful and clear with each other. There should be nothing we can't tell each other."

"Well," I said. "I'm not sad Sally's dead. I certainly didn't feel any animosity toward her, although I didn't like that she was upsetting you. But I'm so sorry it had to happen in your B and B."

"Surprisingly, I feel rather sad, not so much for the Sally who appeared in our lives two days ago, but for the Sally I fell in love with ten years ago. She was so full of life. I guess it's hard to imagine her completely gone."

"I know how that feels."

He pulled me in tight and we had a gentle kiss. Then he held me away just enough so he could look down at me and say, "Let's get out of here. I have another shop that's up for lease that I would like to show you. Then let's go out to dinner. I think not Italian. How about Chinese?"

I went up to our room and changed my clothes, not that they were inappropriate, but I wanted to get rid of the police station smell in them. I scrubbed my face, combed my dark hair back, put on enough makeup to add some color to my cheeks, applied a soft shade of lipstick, and then grabbed a scarf I had bought a few days ago—a Laura Ashley with a rose print on it.

When I came down the stairs, Caldwell was standing at the bottom, patiently waiting for me. "There. You look lovely. Is that a new scarf?"

"Yes, I bought it when I arrived." I was so surprised he noticed. Truly an unusual man.

"This shop we're going to look at today is more out of the way but very reasonable," he told me as we climbed into his smart car.

"Where is it?" I asked.

He paused a moment, then said, "Newington Butts."

"What a wonderful name," I said, adding it to my growing list of weird and wonderful London place names. Spitalfields was still at the top, but Newington Butts was awfully good. "What exactly is a butt?"

"Well, I'd say it is just a stray piece of land, a corner of a field that abuts something else. Thus, the butts."

The drive took us past Westminster Palace. We both saluted as we drove by, Caldwell mentioning that he believed Parliament was in session. Even though I knew that much of the building had been renovated in the late 1800s, the palace still seemed to have come from the Middle Ages.

"Have you ever visited Westminster?" I asked.

"Of course. Every child of London makes many school

visits. And we learn all about the rules and traditions of the place. My favorite one is that no one may eat or drink in the chamber. However, the exception to this rule is that the chancellor of the exchequer—you know, the accountant cabinet member—may have an alcoholic drink while delivering the budget."

"As well he should. That's one difficult job," I said, thinking of going over the finances of the small library I worked at and what a headache it could give me. Maybe a drink was the answer.

After driving over the Westminster Bridge and swirling through a very busy roundabout with cars whizzing by us as if in a tilt-a-whirl, we arrived at the street we were looking for: Iliffe Yard, which featured an artists' cooperative. Actually, the shop we were looking for was right around the corner and was still being run as a millinery goods shop.

When we walked into the very small storefront, I feared we would be suffocated by trim and ribbons. The walls were covered, floor to short ceiling, with boxes of buttons and rolls of fabric.

At first there appeared to be no one there, but as we moved farther back into the store, we saw a small, oldish woman perched on a high wingback chair and sewing something. Her feet didn't touch the floor, and she swung them back and forth as she sewed.

"Hello," I said quietly, not wanting to startle her.

"Yes, yes. Just a minute, just a minute. Let me finish this seam."

Her face was like a well-worn chamois cloth, soft with the fuzz of old age. She made the last stitch, brought the thread up to her mouth, and snapped it off with her teeth. It hurt my mouth to see her cut the thread that way.

When she looked up from her work, her blue eyes were like jewels in her soft face. "What can I help you with today?" she asked.

Caldwell said, "Mrs. Gubbins?"

"That's right." She nodded.

"We've come to see about the shop."

"Oh, yes. My son is forcing me to sell this place and I suppose you're in cahoots with him."

"Not at all. I've never met your son. Just spoke with him by phone. He suggested I come to see you."

"Well, I don't want to go."

I looked around. I could see why she didn't want to leave. How would it ever be possible to undo this feathered nest she had created, where she perched in the deep center like a small bird on its eggs?

"Oh, I'm so sorry," I couldn't stop myself from saying.

"It's not your fault. Would you like a cup of tea?" she asked. She had to slip off the chair to let her feet touch the floor and, instead of growing taller when she stood, she actually shrank. "It's about that time."

I had noticed that wherever you went in England, it was almost always teatime.

"That would be lovely," I said, even though Caldwell shot me a look.

While she went away, we turned around in a circle, taking in the crammed and cramped quarters. The place couldn't have been much larger than the small bedroom on Caldwell's first floor, but there was much about it I liked: the coziness, the south-facing front window, the worn wooden floor scattered with old Persian rugs.

"This won't do," he whispered to me.

"Let's just see what she has to say," I suggested. "Maybe there's a back area. She's obviously gone someplace."

"Go see," he said.

I walked back to the small door she had gone through, knocked, and waited a moment before pushing it open. I found myself in an even smaller room that was obviously the toilet. Mrs. Gubbins was heating water in a plug-in kettle. A tray with a teapot and a plate of biscuits was perched on the sink.

"Won't be but a minute," she said as she poured the hot water into the pot.

"Thanks," I said as I watched her maneuver in the small space.

"Your man seems to have his head on right," she observed.

I was glad to hear it was so obvious. "I think he does," I told her. Then I backed out, as there was no room to turn around.

An hour later, we found a Chinese restaurant not far from Mrs. Gubbins's store. The interior glowed in red and gold and smelled of soy sauce and garlic. I found I was famished.

After ordering a beer, and before ordering our food, Caldwell said, "Absolutely not. The place is simply too small."

"But you said yourself the price was right."

"It would take months to get her to agree to leave, then years to sort out that place. Plus, it's considerably too small."

I knew he was right. "I won't argue."

"How unlike you," he said, and smiled.

"I know you're right, but I just liked the feel of the place. So cozy, so intimate. But I admit, not much room for your thousands of books. And since it will be your shop, you must be comfortable with it."

"We must be sensible," he said, and then stopped. "However, I do think of it as *our* place."

"Oh, Caldwell, we agreed that I would have this trip to decide about all that."

"But you've been here two weeks. Even though it feels

like just a moment. Other than the horrible demise of Sally, and I know it's hard to see around that happening, haven't we been doing well?"

I reached out and touched his cheek. "Yes, more than well. But I won't be rushed. My indecision really isn't about us."

"Then what?" he asked.

He deserved the best explanation I could give him. "I haven't had much luck in relationships before. Maybe I'm just protecting myself, but I want to be sure that I can be happy here in London before I commit. How horrible it would be for you and for me if I came to live here, only to find that it just wouldn't work."

He closed his eyes.

I reached out and touched his cheek. "I couldn't bear that to happen and neither could you."

"Yes, I see."

"Plus, this horrible Sally affair must be settled. You could still end up not owning all of the bed-and-breakfast."

"That's an awful thought."

"But one we must face. If Sally left no will and if her legal claim turns out to be legitimate, then her half might well go to Penelope."

"Yes, Penelope said she was checking into that. I guess there is a solicitor who their family always used. Maybe she'll have some news for us when we get home. At the very worst,

I would only own half of it, but that should still be enough for us to move forward with our plans."

"And when they find out what happened to Sally?"

"The inquest will resolve that," Caldwell said with a deep certainty that I did not feel.

SIXTEEN

In Question

"This is horrible. I can't believe we have to go through this," Caldwell said as he fastened the top button on his suit coat.

"I know, but the inquest will be over soon. Maybe then we'll know what happened, or at least what the police suspect," I told him, stepping in closer to adjust his tie. I had rarely seen him so dressed up: a suit and a tie—he looked mighty handsome, if rather somber.

I wasn't as dressed up, but I wore my one dark skirt, a peasant blouse, and a light cotton sweater—even though it was a warm day, I knew those public rooms could be over-air-conditioned.

"Karen, all an inquest does is ascertain how the deceased came to be dead—it does not try to establish who might be guilty."

"Oh, so we won't learn anything we don't already know?"

"We must wait and see."

Almost everyone in the B and B was going to be at the inquest: Penelope as the closest of kin, Alfredo as Sally's lover (he didn't quite fit into the category of civil partner yet), and the rest of us as concerned persons and witnesses.

Bruce, since he had slept through most of the event and had never even met Sally, was not going. The police had not deemed his presence necessary. This morning, as per usual, he'd headed out bright and early with his list of bookshops to visit, and I would be surprised to see him before nightfall.

Alfredo and Penelope had left right after breakfast, even though the inquest didn't start until ten thirty.

Caldwell insisted that Brenda ride with us. She was wearing a clean but dowdy-looking shirtwaist dress. She had pulled her hair back tight, which I thought gave her face a squinched look. She looked more like a librarian than I did. As we walked out the door, she avoided looking at me. I wondered, as I often did, why she hadn't warmed to me.

We had decided to take a cab so we wouldn't have to try to find parking, which, according to Caldwell, was getting harder and harder even though they had passed the tariff for cars going into the City.

Caldwell held the door of the cab for me. I slid across on the backseat. Then Brenda climbed in and sat on the jump seat, and Caldwell slid in next to me. He gave the driver the address and off we went.

"I've never been to an inquest," I said, trying to be conversational. "Have either of you?"

"For my auntie," Brenda murmured.

"Oh dear. Why? What happened to her?" I asked.

"She died," Brenda revealed.

"Under unusual circumstances?"

"She choked," Brenda said.

"On what?" Caldwell asked.

"Turned out it was a peach pit," Brenda said. "That's what the autopsy report said. But I didn't even know she liked peaches."

"I'm so sorry," I said.

"Wouldn't have been so bad if it would have been something she liked. She loved oranges, but kind of hard to choke on an orange pip."

I grabbed Caldwell's hand but didn't look at him. He squeezed hard, and we both managed not to break out laughing. The ride was short and quiet.

When we got to the Laws Court building, we were directed by a signpost to the basement. Somehow it seemed right that, like the autopsy, the inquest should take place in the bowels of the building.

It was a small gathering in the courtroom. The coroner presided and started by calling Inspector Blunderstone to the stand.

The inspector told the coroner what he had found on arriving at the scene: "A forty-two-year-old woman named Sally Burroughs was lying on the floor of a library surrounded by books. The room was located on the second floor of a house that was being run as a B and B."

"Was she dead when you arrived?" the coroner asked.

"Yes, quite dead, sir."

"How was this determined?"

"The paramedics had tried to resuscitate her and called her death at around four A.M. That was a good half an hour before I came on the scene. So I think it was safe to assume that she was very dead."

"When you arrived what were you told had happened?"

"That after a loud crash, said woman, Sally Burroughs, had been found under a bookcase full of books, which had fallen on top of her, so to speak."

"Indeed. And is that what it looked like to you?"

"Yes, it did. However, in order to help the woman, the books and the bookcase had been taken off her, you know, to see if she was still alive. So I didn't actually see her under the books."

"Very good." The coroner looked down at his desk, then asked, "Were you able to ascertain how the bookcase had come to fall?"

"Yes, it appears that the hook which attached said bookcase to the wall had been unhooked."

"So it fell by itself?"

"It might have, but I rather doubt it. The bookcase stood in front of an old-fashioned door that led to the hallway and was locked. But this door had a transom at the top, which is where they are usually located, and this transom could have been pushed open and thus the bookcase could have been pushed from the hallway, if you see what I mean."

"I do indeed," the coroner stated. "Please continue."

"Well, I don't mean to repeat myself, but the top of the bookcase stood right in front of the transom, and the door itself was about six feet tall, so anyone who was tall enough or had use of a stool or ladder could have pushed with enough force to cause the bookcase to topple."

"So what you're saying is that someone might have caused the bookcase to fall and killed the poor woman?"

"Yes, that is a distinct possibility."

After thanking the inspector for his time, the coroner called Penelope Burroughs to the stand.

"What is your relationship with the deceased?"

"I am, I mean, I was her sister. I guess I still am."

"Are you the closest of kin?"

"In a way. There is my mother, I guess she might be closer, but she's not very compos mentis."

The coroner looked at her, his eyebrows sinking down over his eyes. "She's not very what?"

"She's very muddled. She seems to forget from time to time that Sally has died. So I didn't think she should come to this."

"Yes, I see. Did you find your sister in the library?"

"No, I think it was Caldwell, the owner of the B and B. He was my sister's significant other for many years, and he's a really nice man. I think he was the first one to find her."

"Was anyone else there?"

"Yes, that woman," and here Penelope pointed to me. "Karen Nash. She was already in the library when I came in."

"Did you take the books off your sister's body?"

"I think I helped. It's all rather a blur, but I would have helped, wouldn't I have? You see we hoped that she was still all right even though it didn't look very good. There wasn't really any blood or anything. Just so many books. And she was lying so still, never moved."

Next was Caldwell. He squeezed my hand as he stood to take the stand. I squeezed back and off he went. I knew he was nervous as he didn't like speaking in public much.

"State your full name."

"Caldwell Perkins, sir."

"Mr. Perkins, you are the owner of the B and B where the deceased was residing at the time of her death."

"Yes, she was one of my guests."

"But you had known her previously?"

"Yes, for several years. Sally and I had run the B and B together."

"You were on good terms with her?" the coroner asked, looking over his reading glasses.

"Actually, sir, I was on no terms with her—neither good nor bad. I hadn't spoken to her in nearly seven years."

"And why is that?"

"She ran off on me."

"Were you upset by this?"

"Yes, I was at the time. Surprised, but also rather relieved."

"Why?"

"Sally didn't like running the B and B, and she made her feelings clear. I was doing most of the work anyway, and so it was actually easier after she left."

"But now she came back and wanted to reclaim her ownership."

"That's what she said."

"How did you feel about that?"

"Again, surprised to see her after all this time, but willing to work something out. I was planning a change of careers myself."

"To what?"

"A bookseller."

"This is why you had so many books?"

"Yes, sir."

"How many books do you have?"

Caldwell's eyes met mine. He admitted, "Four thousand three hundred and twenty-four."

"Hmm. And they were all in this room?"

"Most of them."

"Were they on sturdy bookcases?"

"Yes, the bookcases were made to carry such loads, solid oak. I had them made to order."

"And had one ever fallen over before?" the coroner asked.

"No, I was careful about that. As has been established, I had them attached to the walls with hooks. It's an old house and the floors aren't exactly level, but I shimmed the bottoms of the bookcases and attached them to the walls. So, they shouldn't have fallen over—even if they had been unhooked."

"Had you unhooked them from the walls?"

"No, sir. I hadn't done that."

"Did you ever unhook them?"

"No, sir. I didn't. No need." He hesitated, then continued. "That's not quite right. I might have unhooked one to move the bookcase, but that was long ago."

The coroner told him he could step down.

Next up was Alfredo. Before even being asked he announced who he was. "My name is Alfredo Remulado von Savoy."

"My," said the coroner. "That's a good mouthful of a name. Where are you from?"

"But of course Italy."

"How did you know Sally Burroughs?"

"I was sleeping with her," Alfredo announced.

"So you were with her the night she died?"

"I was in bed with Sally that night."

"Do you know why she got up and went to the library?"

"I don't know. She wanted to read, maybe."

"I see from the pathologist's autopsy report that her blood alcohol was rather high. Had you been drinking a lot?"

"Yes, we have much wine with dinner. A celebration."

"What were you celebrating?"

"To be in England, you know. Sally was happy to be home. She had not been for a very long time."

"How did you come to find Sally that night?"

"I hear this screaming so loud from that woman." He pointed at Brenda. "I can't stand it. I get up and go to the hall and see there are people in the library. I go there and my Sally is on the floor. She had died." Here Alfredo looked at the coroner and said, "You know I had loved her very much."

After Alfredo, I was called to the stand. I must admit it

felt odd to be in front of all the people who had been at the scene of the crime and repeat what I was fairly sure everyone in the room already knew. Possibly even the coroner.

But I told him my name, mentioned I was a librarian from Sunshine Valley, Minnesota, and said that I was considering a move to England to be with Caldwell Perkins.

"Describe what happened the night of Ms. Burroughs's demise, please," the coroner asked of me.

"Sally came to the B and B that afternoon. Both Caldwell and I were surprised by her appearance, since the room was registered under Mr. Remulado's name and we had no idea she was coming. She told us her plans . . ." I paused.

"And they were what?" the coroner prodded.

"That she wanted to reclaim her part of the B and B and that she was back to stay."

"How did you feel about this?"

"Well, I thought it was grossly unfair to Caldwell. After all, he had been running the business for years without her. And when she had deserted him she said that he could have the B and B."

"Were you upset about this?"

"I'd say more stunned and confused. I don't always understand the way things work in this country, and I wasn't sure what this all could mean for Caldwell."

"Then what happened?"

"Well, as you heard, Alfredo and Sally went out for dinner and came back fairly late. Caldwell and I were sleeping, but I woke when they came up the stairs because they were so loud."

"Why were they so loud? Were they fighting?"

"No, nothing like that. They were laughing and stumbling about. They sounded very drunk. Then I fell back to sleep and I was awakened by a loud crash that sounded quite near. When I sat up in bed, I saw that Caldwell wasn't there and I was scared that something had happened to him."

"Why did you assume that?"

"I wasn't thinking logically. Just where my mind went in the middle of the night."

"What did you do?"

"I jumped out of bed, opened the door, and saw Caldwell standing in the doorway of the library. He looked horrified."

"Had he already been in the room?"

Oh, how I wished I could answer with any certainty that he hadn't been. But I had to speak the truth. "I really couldn't tell, but it appeared that he had only just come up to the door and looked in."

"But there was no way for you to know this," the coroner insisted.

"No," I admitted.

Brenda was the next witness, but she wasn't much help. She was crying so hard she could barely say her own name.

When she had wiped her face and settled her tears, the coroner asked her what she knew.

"I came up the stairs from my room, which you know is on the main floor. I even have my own bathroom, right next to the garden room. Quite cozy." She hiccuped a last sob.

"I'm sure. What did you see?"

"Well, they were all standing around, and it didn't look good for Sally. Then the medic guys came and said she was dead. I couldn't believe it, I really couldn't. Not Sally."

"In your job as cleaning lady, did you ever notice if the bookcases were unhooked from the walls?"

"No, I wasn't really allowed in that room very often. Caldwell always said he'd dust it himself. Very particular he was about those books."

"So you never went in the library?"

"Once in a while I did. To wash the floor, you know. Maybe every couple of months. It didn't get very dirty since no one hardly went in there, except for him. That room was always kept locked." She nodded in Caldwell's direction.

When the coroner told her she could step down, she stood up, then pointed a finger at me. "But it's all her fault. Whatever happened to Sally. If that woman wouldn't have come, everything would be like it was. Sally would still be alive."

SEVENTEEN

꘏

The Final Witness

I couldn't believe what I had heard Brenda say. I knew she
had never liked me—maybe because I was American, maybe
because she was jealous of my relationship with Caldwell. I
had always been so careful not to tell her what to do or to get
in her way. But I had never been able to please her.

Caldwell stood and addressed the coroner in a loud
voice. "That is a ridiculous accusation. Karen had nothing to
do with Sally in any way. Why, she had only just met her that
afternoon."

"Please come to order," the coroner demanded.

I took Caldwell's hand and pulled him down by my side.

"We'll have a fifteen-minute recess and then hear the last witness."

Brenda ran out of the courtroom before anyone else. No one went after her. I certainly didn't know what to say to her. Caldwell and I walked out of the room slowly as people stared at both of us.

Just to get away from the eyes, I slipped into the restroom. I looked at myself in the mirror. What had just happened? It felt as if I'd been accused of murdering a woman I didn't even really know.

I washed my face and dried my hands, then renewed my lipstick. My face was rather wan, but that dash of rosy pink helped.

The doors of the stalls looked inviting. Just slipping behind one, closing the door, and reading while the inquest went on sounded like such a good idea.

As I never went anywhere without one, I did have a book in my purse. But as tempting as it was to go into a stall and close the door behind me, then sit and read a few pages of Karen Armstrong's terrific memoir *The Spiral Staircase,* I resisted. Caldwell had defended me, and he needed me now.

He was waiting for me right outside the door. "I'm so sorry about that, Karen."

"Oh, we're all on edge. I understand Brenda wanting to take it out on me. I know how bad she feels about Sally's death."

"No excuse," he said. We reached out for each other's hands and walked back into the courtroom.

After a few minutes of everyone filing back into the room, the coroner returned to the throne he sat in and called the last witness. "Would Dr. Steinbeck please take the stand?"

The doctor came forward from where he had been sitting at the back of the room. I hadn't noticed him before, but then he exemplified the word *nondescript*: a small gray man in a gray suit, with gray hair. And with him gray meant "no color at all."

"Dr. Steinbeck, what is your occupation?"

"I'm a forensic examiner specializing in dactyloscopy."

"That is?" the coroner asked.

"I analyze the impressions left by the friction ridges of a human finger. In other words, fingerprints. I analyze fingerprints."

"And in this case where did you find fingerprints that you could analyze?"

"I was brought in to look for latent fingerprints specifically on two items of interest: the hook on the top of the bookcase and the bookcase itself."

"And did you find fingerprints?"

"Yes, I did, sir. Yes, using a Kelvin probe scan, which is able to pull prints off of rounded surfaces, I found partial fingerprints on both objects."

"And did they match any fingerprints to your knowledge?"

He nodded solemnly. "Yes, they matched exemplar prints that had been made at the scene of the crime."

I remembered us all lining up to have our fingerprints done. I had been surprised by how much of the fingers they printed, not just the tip but almost the whole finger. I wondered what name he was about to say.

"Whose?" the coroner asked, leaning forward.

"There was a nice slice of a print on the hook, and then I got a larger print off the back of the bookcase. In my estimation both of them came from the same person."

"Yes?" the coroner urged.

"Caldwell Perkins."

"No." The word popped out of my mouth.

Next to me Caldwell put his face in his hands. An audible gasp came out of several people sitting near us. I couldn't tell who.

"What do you make of this?" the coroner asked.

"I can say no more than it is probable that Mr. Perkins was the last person to have touched these two objects."

EIGHTEEN

An Arresting Moment

On the ride home from the inquest, Caldwell and I held hands. We talked of little, both of us shocked by what he had just been through. I wanted to reassure him, but I wasn't sure I could find the words.

When we drove up to Caldwell's house, he dropped my hand as we saw a police car sitting in front of it.

"Not already," he said with force.

"We must help them all we can so this inquisition will be over sooner," I said. "Don't worry. They might have come to tell us good news, maybe officially declaring Sally's death an accident."

When we walked in the door, Inspector Blunderstone clomped down the hallway toward us with heavy, authoritative steps. He nodded, and the cop standing by the door pounced on Caldwell, seizing him by both hands.

"I'm afraid we're taking you in, Mr. Perkins," the inspector said, while not looking one bit afraid. I wanted to kick him in the shins. "I'm formally placing you under arrest."

"For what?" I asked, while wondering what an informal arrest looked like.

The inspector turned toward me as if he couldn't quite recall who I was. "For the murder of Ms. Burroughs . . ."

As he was speaking, the constable was putting handcuffs on Caldwell.

"Is this really necessary?" Caldwell asked, looking back at his hands.

"Just a precaution, sir. Very routine."

"I'd hate the neighbors . . ." Before he could say anything more, a wail came from down the hallway.

Brenda walked up behind the inspector, yowling, "He's the best man there is. He hasn't done nothing wrong at all."

Behind her came Penelope, who had her hands up near her mouth as if to stifle a similar sound.

"But on what grounds?" I asked.

The inspector stopped for a moment and said, "It has been determined that the bookcase could not have fallen over by itself. As Mr. Perkins's fingerprints were on both the

bookcase and the unhooked hook, I'm arresting him on sus-
picion of murder."

"Maybe Sally pulled the bookcase over on herself," I suggested, desperate to keep them from taking Caldwell away.

"I'm afraid not. Her fingerprints were not found anyplace
on the front of the bookcase. Just yours and Caldwell's were
found. As was to be expected."

When it became obvious that Caldwell was going to be
trundled off in this most undignified manner, he turned to
me and said, "Can you manage this place on your own?"

"I won't be on my own," I assured him. "I'll have Brenda
to help me and we'll do fine. Don't worry about that at all.
And we'll have you out in a jiffy. Should I call your lawyer?"

"Yes. His number is written on the wall in the kitchen
under emergency numbers. Mr. Clotworthy Prentiss-Hipp."

"I'm sure I'll find it." I was trying to stay calm for
Caldwell's sake, but inside an earthquake was shaking loose
my innards.

Caldwell leaned toward me as if he wanted to give me a
kiss before he was taken away, but the constable pulled him
back and turned him around. The inspector fell in behind
him, and I stood back with Penelope and Brenda.

The constable pushed the door open, and led Caldwell
down the steps and into the street. It was everything I
could do to stop myself from running after him, beating on
the constable, and trying to get Caldwell away from this

madness. But I restrained myself and stood silent until he was seated in the police car and it drove off.

Then I broke down. It might not have been obvious to the two women standing with me, but Rosie would have known I was falling apart. I was having trouble breathing and my hands were clenched tight together.

In my mind I was saying over and over again, "It will be all right. It will be all right," a mantra I always used when I knew it might not be all right. For some reason, the statement still seemed to work.

I took a couple of deep breaths, turned, and asked my companions what had happened.

"Well, the inspector came in and went upstairs before I could stop him, then . . ." Brenda said.

"I had just arrived home before you," Penelope explained.

I held up my hand and said, "Stop. One at a time. But first let's go into the garden room and sit down."

"I'll make tea," Brenda suggested.

As much as I didn't want another cup of tea, I nodded my head. She needed something to do.

"While you're doing that, I'll call the lawyer. Penelope, why don't you turn on the fire?"

I followed Brenda into the kitchen. She hustled about heating the water and getting out the teapot. I read through many telephone numbers written on the wall until I finally found the lawyer's name in Caldwell's familiar scrawl.

I dialed the number, hoping that the gentleman would be home.

"Clotworthy Prentiss-Hipp speaking," a man's slight voice answered.

"Yes, this is Karen Nash. You don't know me, but I'm calling for Caldwell Perkins. He needs you. He's in trouble."

There was a silence on the other end of the line. "I'm sorry," the voice said, tentatively.

"Yes, I am too. But that's the way it is. It's about his old partner in his business, Sally Burroughs. She died here in the house. Books fell on her. Then there was an inquest and now he's gone." I knew I wasn't being very coherent, but the words seemed to pour out of me on their own.

There was silence on his end of the line, then he said, "I still don't understand why you've called me."

"Caldwell Perkins, your client, has been arrested for murder," I said as plainly as I could.

"Oh," Clotworthy Prentiss-Hipp said quietly, "that's not good."

NINETEEN

The Actual Killer

"It's all my fault," Brenda wailed when we all were finally seated in the garden room, the teapot and cups perched on the small coffee table.

I took over pouring the tea since I didn't trust her to do it without spilling, the state she was in. The sound of her voice was making all my nerves jangle. I had to calm her down or I would be forced to hit her.

"What's your fault?" I asked in my calmest voice. I hoped Brenda would parrot me in answering.

"Them finding those fingerprints, it's all my fault," she said as if that explained something.

"How so?" I said, handing around the cups of tea.

"I must not have dusted that room as good as I should have."

"Well, no one could have expected you to take care and dust the hook or the back of the bookcase," I said, trying to comfort her.

"I should have done a better job. Wiped down everything in that room, then Caldwell wouldn't be going to jail. I still think it's all my fault."

"That's bonkers," I said, my voice rising slightly. "What can they be thinking? If Caldwell had pushed the bookcase over, he would have worn gloves. Or done something to obliterate the prints. He's a very smart man. But the most important thing is he absolutely didn't do it. No way."

Penelope spoke up. "I agree with you. But the police don't know him like we do. So many murderers are so sloppy these days."

I was surprised to hear her talk like this.

She continued. "There's really very few clever killings anymore. Or maybe there were never many, except the ones you read about in good mystery books. Most murderers are stupid and drunk. And almost always the murderer is related to the victim in some way."

"How do you know all this?" I asked, suddenly very curious about Penelope's background.

"I worked for the police as a secretary. Husbands beating on their wives while they were drunk was the usual way it went. Stupid bugger often didn't even know he had killed her until the police showed up. Then he was ever so sorry." Penelope took a sip of tea and said "Ta" to Brenda for the refreshment.

"Alfredo seems to fit that description of the typical murderer to a T," Brenda piped in. "Drunk and not so smart and related to Sally by means of being her boyfriend. He's probably who did it."

"He is too smart—in his own way, a rather Italian way, I'd say," Penelope argued. "He just doesn't speak English that well yet. And he doesn't drink that much, not compared to other Italians."

"But he was drinking that night," I observed. "By the way, where is he right now? Is Alfredo still here?"

"Not at the moment. He went out to buy something to wear to the funeral," Penelope said. "But I don't think he had anything to do with my sister's death. He's too nice, and besides, he liked her. He had no reason to want her dead."

"What about her will? Do you know who will inherit Sally's estate, such as it is?" I asked.

"Last I heard, it was to be split between Mum and me. But possibly Sally had changed that. When I asked him, Alfredo didn't seem to know anything about it, and didn't seem to really care. He owns acres of land in Italy."

"Land doesn't necessarily translate into money," I pointed out. "Often keeping up land requires money."

Penelope seemed to be getting upset about the possibility that Alfredo might be responsible for her sister's death, which intrigued me.

She started to say, "Alfredo . . ."

Just at that moment, he walked into the room with a suit wrapped in plastic hanging over his arm. "I do the best I can for the suit. I'm not used to buying this from the rack. Usually my tailor makes them for me."

Penelope looked up and smiled. "I'm sure it will be fine."

"Caldwell has been arrested. They suspect that he murdered Sally," I said, wanting to see Alfredo's reaction to this news. However, in saying these words, I found myself close to tears.

"No, this is not possible. Sally says he is a very nice man. I think so too. This is very crazy."

I was glad to hear Alfredo so confident that Caldwell wouldn't have done it; and I found myself agreeing that this country, which in the past I had always thought of as one of the sanest in the world, the absolute bastion of civility, had gone a little nuts to think for a second that Caldwell might have killed anyone. He would be capable of dumping a cup of tea in someone's lap, possibly, but push a bookcase over he wouldn't do, not in a million years.

I stood up. "It simply can't be Caldwell. He would never have risked damaging any of his books that way."

Brenda nodded agreement and dabbed at her eyes; Penelope said, "You're so right"; and Alfredo shrugged his shoulders and said, "Sally says he loves those books very much always."

"Alfredo, I know you've been asked this before, but do you have any idea why Sally got up in the middle of the night and went into the library?"

"Perhaps it is that she could not sleep. Books always make her very sleepy, especially the boring ones."

I wasn't convinced, but saw no point in arguing with him. He sat down on the love seat next to Penelope, and a look passed between them that seemed somehow intimate.

I decided then and there to find out who had done Sally in. Caldwell's abduction was not to be tolerated. I had to get him out of jail, and it seemed like the only way to do that was to determine who did push the bookcase over.

But I also decided not to announce my decision to these three people, as I had a distinct feeling that one of them was the actual killer.

TWENTY

᎐᠆ᦈᦈ᠆᎐

The Teapot

Because Caldwell was incarcerated, the next day I had to attend Sally's funeral alone. Absolutely everything seemed wrong with this picture: I didn't know the woman very well, I hadn't liked her the little I had known her, and, because of her unfortunate death, my darling Caldwell was locked up in jail and might stay there for a good long time.

But I knew that police often go to the funerals—to gather clues, to see who shows up, to possibly show their respect—and since everyone else in the house, except Bruce, was going, I thought it best if I went too. Who knew what I might discover at this event? Plus, it would be good to do it for Caldwell's sake—it was what he would have wanted me to do.

I hadn't had time to have flowers sent, so I stopped off at a florist's early in the morning and bought a bouquet of white lilies. I knew Sally had loved lilies because there were still so many growing in the garden she had planted at the B and B. White seemed a good color; after all, in many cultures it was the color of mourning.

Penelope had gone out early that morning, but as she was leaving she had told me the service would be at Dratt-Brinkwater and Lyme's funeral home, and that it would be a humanist service. She also added that this was a little unusual—but it was what Sally had wanted.

"Sally was no religion to speak of, except maybe the worship of Sally," she said, and didn't even crack a smile as she said it. In fact, Penelope acted rather sad that the one person who believed in that religion was now gone.

"There will probably only be a small group of us. Mum will come in, and maybe Aunt Doris. Possibly some old friends from school days. I'm not sure."

Alfredo had gone with Penelope. I wasn't sure who was supporting whom, but they seemed fine going off together.

For this trip to London, I had packed no black clothing. Black is not one of my colors, my skin tone is a touch too sallow. I need softer, richer tones to perk up my complexion. But I did have a dark blue blouse, and I paired it with some brown slacks and was glad for the warm weather, which required no jacket.

Just as I was getting ready to set off, I looked in Caldwell's closet and had to sit down on the floor and cry for a few minutes. I hadn't slept at all well the night before, and I certainly wasn't looking forward to this funeral. I had only so many days left here, and I wanted him back with me.

I dug through one of his drawers, found a dark burgundy silk scarf, and tied it around my neck. The scarf looked rather jaunty, and it felt good to have a piece of him with me, and with Sally. I knew Caldwell would have wanted to be at the funeral service. He had rarely spoken badly of Sally, not that she hadn't dumped him in a cruel way, but he had even seen that in a somewhat positive light, saying sometimes those quick breaks are for the best.

Brenda was nowhere to be found when I was ready to go. I had thought we might go together, but after what she had said at the inquest, it might be better if we went separately. My impression was that she had admired Sally a great deal, so I was sure I would see her at the funeral.

I walked by Caldwell's smart car parked on the street but knew I could neither attempt to drive it, especially in London traffic, nor ever find my way around aboveground. The tube was for me. I had marked the closest station to the funeral home and was giving myself plenty of time to find it.

Rubbing the silk of Caldwell's scarf between my fingers, I sighed and set off on my mission.

A tall, thin man in a long, black coat opened the door for me at the funeral home. He looked like a grown-up goth. He intoned that he was Dratt-Brinkwater. On hearing the name said aloud, I switched the two first letters around and then did everything I could do not to laugh. He showed me through to the room where the service would be held.

There were already a few people in the room, but no one I knew. After bringing my bouquet up to set with the other floral arrangements, I sat down on a folding chair in the back. I was glad to see that there was no open casket. In fact, I could see no casket anywhere. Just a large teapot sitting on a pedestal. I then remembered that Sally had been cremated. I wondered if the teapot were for serving refreshments after the service, but it looked more decorative.

Penelope came into the room and walked right over to me. She was wearing a simple black dress, and it suited her, showing off her fair hair and traditional British peaches-and-cream complexion.

"What do you think?" she asked me as she swept her hand toward the front of the room.

"Lovely flowers," I murmured.

"Yes, but the teapot," she said.

Not being sure what I was asked, I responded as genuinely as I could. "It's a very handsome teapot."

"Mum insisted," Penelope told me.

"Oh, she did," I said, still not sure what Sally's sister was telling me.

"Wonderful what they're doing with cremation urns these days, isn't it?" she asked, clasping her hands together.

"Yes," I choked out, finally putting together what the teapot held.

"They even had one that was an exact replica of an old police call box, blue and all. But I thought that would be a little too Doctor Who."

"Yes, I agree," I was comfortable saying. I couldn't help wondering if the ashes could pour out the spout, thus making spreading them that much easier, but I refrained from asking Penelope.

"And here comes Mum. You must meet her. She lives in a nursing home, which is why I'm not staying with her. She's in quite good health, but her mind wobbles. I think she knows what's going on, although she had a hard time at first remembering who Sally was, and I'm not sure she has taken in the fact that she has died. However, she loves funerals."

I stood up and turned around, and for a moment I thought the Queen Mother herself was coming in the door. A short, stout woman, all dressed in black, was wearing a hat that looked like a stovepipe someone had crushed in the front and then added a veil to it. A powder puff of blue-white hair showed beneath the hat.

She held herself very regally and nodded to people as she walked in. Several people stopped to talk to her and hold her hands. She dabbed at her eyes, but smiled and then came our way.

"Mother dear, this is Karen Nash. Karen, this is my mother, Mrs. Burroughs. Mum, Karen is the woman I told you about who is staying at Caldwell's."

"How lovely. And where is that dear man?" she asked.

"I told you, Mum. He couldn't make it but sends his best regards. You know how close he and Sally were."

"Yes, but I did so want to see him. It's been such a long time."

"I'm sure he'll come by for a visit."

Mrs. Burroughs nodded and then looked around with a puzzled expression on her face. "But where is our Sally? She should be here."

Penelope pointed at the teapot. "Remember, Mum. She's in the teapot. She died and we had her cremated."

"Oh, yes, quite right. But I haven't seen her in such a long time. I was so hoping she'd be here."

For an incredulous moment I was sure I was in Wonderland at the Mad Hatter's tea party. Mrs. Burroughs was the Mad Hatter; Penelope, I'm afraid, was Alice; and I was only the March Hare.

Just as I was thinking this, Brenda appeared and we had our dormouse. She had dressed in gray and had pulled her dark hair back tight against her scalp, almost as if she were doing penance. She took Mrs. Burroughs's hand, and I had the sense that she had to stop herself from dropping a curtsy.

"Mrs. Burroughs, I'm so sorry about Sally. She was just too good, and I can't believe she's gone."

"Yes," Mrs. Burroughs said, patting Brenda's hand. "She has been gone for a while now. Italy, I believe."

Brenda dropped Mrs. Burroughs's hand and backed away from her.

Alfredo walked up, and Penelope took his arm. "Mother, I'd like you to meet Alfredo Remulado."

"Oh my. We were just speaking of Italy. *Buon giorno,*" Mrs. Burroughs said.

Ever the Italian, Alfredo didn't just shake her hand, he fussed over it. He seemed a new man—I guess it was the first time I had seen him neither drunk nor hungover. His eyes were clear, his stature distinguished, and his unbespoke clothes fit him to perfection.

Alfredo was, in fact, a very handsome man. Possibly Sally had been his problem. I had to wonder, now that he was rid of Sally, could he bloom into himself?

A few more people wandered in, and we were all asked to be seated by Mr. Dratt-Brinkwater. Some slow and unpleasant hymn was played over the sound system, after which Mr. Dratt-Brinkwater intoned a few words about death being merely a door we step through on a wonderful adventure.

If this was what the humanists believed, I was pleased for them. Not an unpleasant thought. Rather like a quiz game. Choose the right door. Walk on through and maybe a prize will be waiting.

Penelope got up to speak. She held a piece of paper in her hands, of notes I presumed, and while the paper trembled slightly, her voice did not. She too seemed to have grown more into herself.

"My sister and I did not always have the perfect relationship. Sally was forceful, adventurous, and curious. She grabbed on to life as if she intended to throttle it. I admired her for that. She took what she wanted and enjoyed what she got. If something didn't work for her, she tried something else."

Penelope looked down at her notes, and here her voice shook a little as she continued. "And now Sally's gone. It's hard to believe that such a vibrant woman is no longer with us. She will be missed, I'm sure. I will miss my big sister. Maybe more than I can now know."

Next to me Brenda began to sob quietly into her folded hands. I reached into my purse and gave her one of the tissues I always carried with me. As long as I was at it, I pulled out one for myself.

I too felt myself tearing up at the genuineness of Penelope's words. She hadn't tried to make Sally into someone she had not been, someone kind and generous, but in saying who her sister had really been, she made us all miss her some. Those kinds of people do make life more exciting, even if it is sometimes to the detriment of the rest of us. In that moment I wished I had known Sally better.

But what I really wished was that Caldwell was sitting next to me. He was who I really missed.

TWENTY-ONE

Tea for Two

There was no reception following Sally's funeral. There hadn't been many people—Sally having been gone from England for so long—and I guess Penelope just hadn't wanted to fuss with it.

As I was leaving for home, I walked over to say my good-byes and give my condolences to Mrs. Burroughs. She smiled as I said how sorry I was. She thanked me and invited me to tea later that day.

"I'm in a hotel up in Kingsland." She smiled graciously as she added, "You can't miss it. Everyone ends up there at one time or another."

I glanced over at Penelope, who mouthed, "I'll explain."

I smiled and said, "That would be lovely. Might I bring anything?"

"No, the service there is quite nice, and I just thought we could have a little chat. I love to make new friends."

We agreed on a time, and Penelope grabbed my arm and walked outside with me. "Mum's slightly bonkers, but very friendly. You don't have to go. She won't remember she invited you."

"Oh, but I'd like to visit her. The least I can do." As we stood on the steps and basked in the sun, I wondered what the older woman would be able to tell me about her daughters—anything that might shed light on Sally's death. "Do you think she realizes that Sally has died?"

"Occasionally. But then it slips her mind. It's just as well. She would be terribly upset if she had to remember such things all the time." Penelope gave me directions to the "hotel," which turned out to be a senior assisted-living home called Queensland, in Kingsland.

I took the tube back to the B and B and called to see if Caldwell's lawyer had any news.

He answered his phone with the usual announcement of his name, of which he seemed terribly proud.

I couldn't help it. I gave him back the full majesty of my own name. "This is Karen Elizabeth Nash calling."

"I beg your pardon," he said.

I wasn't sure why he was begging my pardon, but I plowed ahead. "I'm calling about Caldwell Perkins."

"Oh, yes, you're that American." This statement he made with a tone that insinuated he'd rather be holding a rat by the tail than having much to do with me. "I thought you might be calling."

"Where are things at?" I asked, eager for news.

"Miss Nash, I'm pleased to say that they are progressing."

I was getting impatient. "How so?"

"I've been in touch with the court and they will be recommending bail."

"Do you have any idea how much that might be?"

"No. But I think we will be advised later today."

It was at times like this that I was glad for the royalty checks I was earning on the invention of the toilet I had helped create: the Flush Budget. Before I left Minnesota, I had set up with my bank a line of credit that I could draw on easily. I told Mr. Prentiss-Hipp that I had access to a fair amount of money in the U.S., and he said that might come in handy.

"Well, let me know as soon as you know anything."

"Miss Nash, I know many things—but any news pertaining to Mr. Caldwell I will keep you apprised of."

"Give him my love," I said.

"Yes, quite," he said, and we rang off.

*   *   *

"Brenda?" I knocked on her door and thought I heard a rustling inside, so I knocked again.

When she came to the door, she looked as if she had continued crying after she left the funeral.

"How are you doing?" I asked.

"Touch of a cold, I think. Besides which I just can't believe Sally's gone."

"Yes, I know."

"What do you know about it?" she said in a nasty voice. "You have no idea what a loss Sally is to many of us."

Not wanting to argue with her, I quickly told her what I needed to. "Listen, I'm going out for a while. Can you attend to things here?"

She huffed. "Of course I can. We were doing fine before you came along. Who do you think took care of things when he went off on his book-buying binges? You've just encouraged that in him. I was often left in charge, and I can run this place just fine."

"Yes, of course you can. I didn't mean to suggest that you couldn't handle things, but was just wondering if you were up to it after the funeral and all."

"Where are you off to anyway?" she asked. "Going to see Caldwell?"

"I wish. No, I'm going to visit Sally's mother. She asked me to tea at the place where she's living."

"She used to be sharp as a whistle, that one. But now she's just whistling an empty tune."

"Yes, she does seem slightly out of it."

"Don't pay much attention to what she says," Brenda advised. "She does like to prattle on."

"No, I just thought it would be nice to visit her."

"She never understood Sally."

I waited to see if Brenda would tell me more. Finally, I nudged, "How so?"

"Just the kind of life Sally was meant for: nice things, lots of travel, carefree, not tied down. Her mum wanted her to marry Caldwell."

"Well, for my sake, I'm glad that she didn't."

Brenda huffed again and then shut the door in my face. I didn't seem to know what to say to please that woman.

The Queensland in Kingsland was not very royal. Looked more like Disneyland without the spires: fake stone on new walls, patterned carpeting that mimicked Persian rugs, cheap ceramic pots that had plastic flowers in them.

After inquiring at the front desk, I was told that I would probably find Mrs. Burroughs out on the patio, waiting for her tea.

I strolled through the large hallway, watching one woman

walk herself around in her wheelchair and a man dressed as if he were going out on a hunt, striding up and down the hall. They both seemed fairly happy. I followed the receptionist's directions out the other side of the building and saw a large lawn with a croquet game in progress.

Mrs. Burroughs was sitting next to a table in the shade, by herself, dozing. I walked up to her, and her head jerked up and her eyes opened. "Are you bringing my tea?" she asked hopefully.

"No, but I'm sure it will be here soon." I could see she didn't remember me. "May I sit down?"

"Of course. What's your name, my dear?"

"I'm Karen Nash."

"A good, sensible name," she said.

I nodded. I had always found it so.

"I'm Mrs. Burroughs. You must be new here. How do you like the hotel?" she asked.

"Lovely," I said, looking around at the lawn and the gardens. "Quite lovely."

"Yes," she said. "It's not quite like home, but it will do. I'm not sure how long I'll be staying, you know. But for now it will do."

"I know your daughters," I told her, since it was basically true. Then I reminded her, "Sally and Penelope."

"Oh, how nice. I rarely see them," she said. "You know girls at that age are so busy. But they are good girls mostly."

"How do they get along?" I asked.

"Oh, much the way they should. Sally's quite the stronger of the two. Always has been. Penelope is sweeter, but also I think a little devious. Penelope was always jealous of Sally, always thought she got more attention. But they're good girls. I wish I would see them more often."

"Did they ever quarrel or fight?" I asked.

She rubbed her cheek with her hand as if she were trying to remember something. "I seem to remember some sort of to-do about the ring."

"What ring?"

"Oh, you know, that big sort of flashy ring. I think it was Victorian. Lots of emeralds and diamonds and such. I gave it to Penelope, as she had always loved it, but I think Sally thought she deserved it somehow. Then it went missing. Penelope always said Sally took it, but I don't know. Penelope might have just mislaid it. She could be forgetful sometimes. Personally I didn't care for the ring. I always found it rather ugly."

"It sounds expensive," I said.

"Yes, I suppose. Those things usually are. With all those gaudy stones on it, but not in particularly good taste, if you know what I mean. However, it was the last of our great fortune. You might wonder why I'm staying in this hotel." She swept her hand around at the building. "We lost all our wealth when their father gambled it away. The ring was the last of it, and I couldn't stand to wear it. Just reminded me of better times. You know how it is."

I murmured assent.

Then the tea cart was pushed up to our table by a young girl whose hair color was a little too close to carrot to be natural. "Mrs. Burroughs, what'll you have for your tea today?" she asked.

"I think I'll try one of those sandwiches." She pointed to a triangle of white bread with cucumber slices. "And a scone, please."

The girl handed her a plate with her desired dainties. Then I pointed out several things I wanted and a blop of double cream, a real downfall for me. We both had tea with a dribble of milk.

"I'm a friend of Caldwell's," I told her after we were served. "I've been staying at the B and B."

"Such a lovely man he is. I don't understand why Sally left him. One can only guess. But then we didn't talk about such things." She was silent for a moment, then continued. "But you know she's never married. The young people these days just don't go in for that much."

"Yes, well, Caldwell's in a bit of trouble, having to do with Sally."

Mrs. Burroughs looked up. "Not again."

"How so?" I asked.

"Well, she left him with that mess of a B and B, didn't she? He had to keep it going on his own."

"Yes, I guess she did."

"I've missed him. You should have brought him with you," she said. "I would have loved to see him."

"Yes, I think he would have liked that too."

"I haven't seen much of Sally lately either," she told me. "I wonder what could be keeping her."

I couldn't lie to her, but I said as gently as I could, "Sally had a bad accident and died a few days ago."

Her sandwich dropped from her hand. "Oh, it's not right for children to die before their parents. Did she suffer much?"

"No, I think it happened too quickly for that."

"That's a mercy." She shook her head as if something was bothering her, then began eating her sandwich again. "These sandwiches taste a little dry today. I will have to say something."

I had finished my scone and said, "I'm so sorry about your daughter Sally. It must be such a loss." I couldn't keep myself from saying this even if Mrs. Burroughs didn't understand.

Her face darkened, her eyes fell, as she slowly ate her last bite, and then she said, "I hate to think about it. She was always such a good girl."

TWENTY-TWO

Keep Bailing

The next day I woke up to a lovely dream. I was lying in bed and a gentle hand caressed my face. Then I felt the lightest kiss on my forehead and I heard a voice saying, "I'm so glad to see you, my love."

I opened my eyes, and two big brown eyes were staring at me. It took me a long second to realize it was Caldwell, and then I threw my arms around him, dragging him down on top of me.

We kissed as if we hadn't seen each other for years. As we lay next to each other, I finally was able to speak. "How did you get here?"

"I broke out."

I hoisted myself up on an elbow. "Really?"

"No, I'm out on bail. Remember? You posted it."

"Yes, but Mr. Snotworthy Princess-Drip said it might take days for you to be released."

"Mr. Clotworthy Prentiss-Hipp doesn't like to get one's hopes up. But he can be very effective when he chooses to be."

I had to ask the question I was afraid to hear the answer to. "Do they really think that Sally was killed and it wasn't an accident?"

"Yes, that's what they told me. That a forensic guy looked over the room and the bookcase and determined there was no way for it to have fallen on its own, and Sally couldn't have pulled it over because she was facing away from it when it fell on top of her."

"Oh my," I said as a slightly stronger phrase came to my mind. "And they think you were the one who did it?"

"My handprints are all over the bookcase and I was the first one on the scene. They feel these facts make me the most culpable."

I sat up in bed and said decisively, "Now we must find out who really killed Sally."

Caldwell sat up next to me and said in an equally determined voice, "Karen, I want you to stay out of this. This doesn't involve you, and it could get nasty. Maybe you should go home for a while."

"It's already been nasty—you in jail for days—and it most certainly does involve me. Why, I'm sure I'm one of their suspects, and we need to clear your name. Plus, someone killed Sally, and we need to find out who." I sank down on the pillow next to him. "You don't really want me to go home, do you?"

"No, not very much. I'm just worried."

"But this is just another test of our compatibility. If we get through this, then we'll feel more certain of our relationship."

"Yes, if one of us doesn't end up in jail for a very long time."

"My point exactly. We know neither one of us did it—so all we have to do is find out who did. It can't be that hard. It can only be one of four people who were in the house that night: Alfredo, Penelope, and Brenda. I don't see how Bruce can be a suspect. He knew no one, except you. At the moment, I'm leaning toward Penelope."

"Why?"

"Because of the ring."

"What ring?" he asked, puzzled.

"Did you ever see Sally wear a very ornate Victorian ring with emeralds and diamonds?"

He cocked his head like a robin looking for a worm and pondered, then said, "I remember a ring that Sally liked to flash around once in a while. She called it her cocktail ring. Very gaudy."

"Yes, sounds like the very ring. It had been given to Penelope and, as she feared, Sally took it. Do you know where it is? Did Sally take it with her when she left for Italy?"

"I haven't a clue." He thought for a moment, then asked, "So you think that Penelope killed her sister over a ring? Seems a bit mad. And why now? Why here, of all places?"

"I think the ring might have been the proverbial straw that broke the camel's back. According to their mother, Penelope was awfully jealous of Sally. Why now? Probably because this was the first real opportunity she had when there were other people around that could be blamed—like you."

"Sally's mum told you that? How did you happen to talk to her?"

"I went to see her after the funeral. Just to ask her a few questions."

"Which is exactly what I don't want you to do. This is not your problem, Karen."

"Yes, anything that involves you is my problem. Get used to it."

He smiled and said, "I'd like to."

We kissed again. But Caldwell still had questions. "Penelope visited Sally in Italy. Why not there?"

"Because I don't think the ring was there. Maybe that's what Sally was looking for in the library. Maybe she hid the ring there and was trying to find it."

"There are many maybes in your thesis."

"One has to start somewhere."

He rolled out of bed and stretched. I liked looking at his solid body. Even though he was a book person, he had the body of a healthy farmer, dimpled and hard.

"I'd like to start with breakfast," he said. "How does a real English fry-up sound to you?"

I grabbed my robe. "I feel like I haven't had a decent meal in days."

"I *haven't* had a decent meal in days," he muttered.

"Was it awful?" I asked as we both shuffled down the hallway to the stairs.

"Not my usual clientele. A rough lot they were. But I was treated all right. Just had to wear this gray overall that didn't fit very well."

"Gray isn't one of your best colors."

When we got to the bottom of the stairs, Caldwell took hold of me by the shoulders. "I don't want to go back there."

"You won't. We'll figure this out."

Once in the kitchen Caldwell went to work. So far all he allowed me to do was toast the bread. He had a lovely silver toast rack—the British like their toast cold so it doesn't melt the butter. Don't ask me why they like solid butter. I was getting used to cold toast.

I popped bread slices in the toaster and, when they were done, placed them carefully into the rack while Caldwell fried up some eggs, sausages, bacon, and a tomato. My favorite part was the fried tomato. Plus, it was probably the only thing that was fairly good for me.

"What about our guests?" I asked as we sat down to eat in the kitchen. "What are they going to eat?"

"They'll have to understand that nothing is normal right now. Are they even here? I haven't heard any noise upstairs."

"I'm pretty sure they were here last night. I wasn't in the mood to talk, so I didn't check in with them. I know Penelope wasn't at her mother's because I was there, plus I don't think they allow sleepovers at the old folks' home."

"That's where Mildred is now? At an old folks' home, whatever that is. It sounds awful."

"Mildred? I never got her first name. She's not quite all there these days. It's not such a bad place. She thinks she's staying in a hotel. The hard part is that she doesn't even remember what happened a few hours earlier. I had to remind her of Sally's death."

"I'm sorry to hear that. She must be in her eighties."

"Yes, I'd guess she is. She seems quite happy, but not aware of what's going on. Her short-term memory is shot, but she could remember things from when the girls were young."

Just as we finished up our meals, there was a rather tentative knock on the front door. Caldwell looked down at his robe and then shrugged and went to answer it. I walked behind him. I wasn't letting him out of my sight. I didn't want anyone to take him away from me again.

A rather official-looking man in a long gray coat had an envelope in his hand. "I am to deliver this to a Mr. Alfredo Remulado. Is he lodging here at present? And if so, may I see him?"

"Yes," Caldwell said, reaching for the envelope. "I'll see that he gets it."

"No, this has to be given to him personally."

Just then Alfredo came walking down the hall in his silk pajamas.

"Letter for you, Alfredo," Caldwell told him.

We stepped out of his way, and the man handed him the envelope, then turned and left.

"What is this?" Alfredo asked.

"Open it," I suggested.

He opened it and read. "I'm not sure I understand what it says here for me." He handed the letter to Caldwell, who skimmed the contents quickly, then looked up at Alfredo.

"For what it's worth, Sally made someone named Giuseppe Molto her beneficiary," Caldwell said.

"Giuseppe, that is me." Alfredo threw an arm around Caldwell's shoulder. "Then we will be partners together."

TWENTY-THREE

Changing the Mind

"But on the second thought I don't want it." Alfredo pushed the letter away as Caldwell tried to hand it back to him.

"Why not?" I asked, surprised at his reaction. "And who's Giuseppe?"

"That's my real name. Alfredo my nickname. I cannot be here anymore. I must go back to Italy. I see how much work the B and the B is. It is too much trouble to run such a place as this."

Caldwell took Alfredo's hand and gave him the letter.

"But if, in fact, Sally has a legal claim to the B and B, then I would have to buy you out."

"Buy me out?" Alfredo was puzzled.

"Surely you must understand this, man. I would pay you for your part of the B and B, minus what I'm owed for keeping the place going. You wouldn't have to do anything."

"Oh, that is much better," Alfredo said, smiling and nodding.

"I thought it might be."

"How much would this money be?" Alfredo asked.

"We would have to get the house and business appraised and then also factor in the years that I ran it on my own."

"I understand very little of this."

Penelope walked in off the street, right into the middle of the conversation. She was wearing a flowered dress and looked younger and brighter than I had seen her before. "Hullo, hullo. What's this confab about?"

"I have some news." Alfredo held up the letter and shook it.

"I hope it's good. I need to hear something good," she said, putting down her packages.

"Depends on whose point of view you look at it from," Caldwell said, with some slight glumness.

"Things need to be worked out." I couldn't help but reach out and take hold of his hand.

"Tell me," Penelope said.

"I am sharing this inn with Mr. Caldwell," Alfredo said with delight. "He will pay me some money for it."

Penelope looked askance. "What?"

"What he's trying to say is he just got a letter from Sally's lawyer informing him that he has inherited a share of the B and B," Caldwell said.

"Oh, he did?" Penelope said, and looked rather baffled. "How could that have happened?"

"It is because of Sally. She does it. She does it for me." Alfredo smiled, then added, "Even though I was not always the best for her. Especially now that she is dead. I cannot even thank her."

I couldn't tell if Alfredo was having trouble with the language, was incredibly naïve, or was just a simple soul. Maybe a mixture of all the above. He seemed oblivious to how bad the three of us felt about this news: Caldwell because he would have to deal with Alfredo and lose a share of the money from the B and B, Penelope because her sister had left her nothing, and me because I wanted Caldwell to get it all—as he deserved.

Penelope closed her eyes for a moment, then said, "How nice for you. Excuse me. I need to go upstairs with my things." She picked up her packages and bolted.

"I too have things to attend to, in the kitchen," Caldwell

said, then left me standing in the hallway with the beaming Alfredo.

"I think we might have a drink," he said. "I bought some grappa for everyone to enjoy."

Nice to do after you've cleaned out Caldwell's liquor cabinet, I thought. "Grappa?" I asked.

"It is the best. You will love it. It is made with the leftovers from making the wine. Very good for you."

I followed him into the garden room. I thought Caldwell needed some time alone, plus I was curious about something that Alfredo had let slip.

He opened a very plain bottle with a simple white label. He poured each of us a thimbleful in Caldwell's sherry glasses.

"*Salute,*" he said, and chugged his drink.

Things couldn't get worse, I thought, so I followed suit. The grappa hit my chest like an explosive oomph. My eyes watered, my nose ran, and I started to choke. "Wow!" I managed to exclaim.

"It's very good, no?" Alfredo asked.

"If you like to get blown away."

"Yes, this is good. It opens up the whole body."

When my body had closed up a bit, after I'd wiped my eyes and blown my nose, we sat looking at each other. Alfredo poured himself another drink, but I passed. This was my chance.

"So you mentioned that you weren't always the best for Sally. What did you mean by that?"

"Oh, it's nothing really, but I was going to tell her something on this trip and I never got the chance."

"What?"

"Well, it matters not at all now, because she is gone. As you say, she is passed away. But I did not love Sally as much as before. I had changed in my thinking and in my feeling for her."

"So you didn't want to get married?" I asked, surprised by what he was telling me.

"Not really. Not anymore. This is hard for her to understand because everyone loves Sally for a while. But she is hard to be with for a long time. She is a very . . ." He searched for a word and put his arms out as if encompassing a large ball. "She takes up much space in the world. Sometimes this makes me very tired."

"Yes, I understand. Did you know that she was going to leave you anything?"

"Not really. All I know is she goes to see the lawyer. And I'm deciding that I must tell her about my changing of mind. But it seems not the right thing to do just yet. I can never find the moment."

I wondered what he thought she was going to the lawyer about, if Alfredo was telling the truth about not knowing about the change in the will. "Well, you're a lucky guy."

"I hope so," he said. *"Un altro?"* He lifted up the bottle of grappa.

"No, thank you."

He poured himself another glass. "But I must have one more. One is for me, one for B and B, and one is for my Sally, who was good to me as much as she could be."

TWENTY-FOUR

All Will Be Well

Inspector Blunderstone once again appeared at the door of the B and B the next day, but this time he asked to see Mr. Remulado. When I didn't move for a moment, he explained that he needed to speak to him about the will.

"I'll get him," I said as I could hear that Caldwell was cleaning up the breakfast dishes.

Even though it was nearly nine o'clock, it was still quite early for our Italian guest. I knocked on his door and heard him say, *"Entra."* Walking in, I found Alfredo stretched across the bed, looking as if he were trying to swim to a far shore. I roused him and told him to dress, that he had company.

When he rolled out of bed, I was glad, for my own sense of decency, to see that he was wearing a complete pair of pajamas. I wanted to reach out and feel the fabric, as they had the drape of silk.

"Who is here for me?" he asked.

"The cop."

"What is this . . . cop?"

"Sorry, it's the police, the inspector, he wants to talk to you."

"Still about my Sally," he said.

"Yes, but are you sure she was your Sally?"

"You are right. She belonged to no one."

I left him to throw on some other clothes and led the inspector into the garden room, where Penelope was reading the newspaper, then went to help Caldwell clear up the dishes. He told me that Bruce had already gone out for the day.

"He's really been bugging me to see my collection of books. He's dying to get in the library," Caldwell said.

"Well, why not show it to him?" I picked up a towel and started wiping the dishes he had left to dry.

"I'm just not sure I'm ready. I don't have most of them priced, and I feel like I want to make a grand splash when we open the shop."

I decided to not correct him about the "we" opening the shop. "You've got to sell them sometime," I said. "Wouldn't that help with the cash flow?"

"Yes, but I have to decide what ones I will sell and for how much. It's complicated." His face scrunched up in thought.

I reached out and smoothed his brow. "I see that."

"This is one of the many reasons I need you. I'm so counting on you to help me sort through the books and figure out what's a fair price. I know you have that kind of mind."

I smiled. "You are such a sweet talker. How many men know to compliment a woman on her mind?"

Suddenly we heard a skirmish going on in the hallway. When we looked out the kitchen door, the inspector was leading Alfredo away, but Penelope was trying to hold him back.

"He needs someone else to be there. I'm going with him," she said.

"No, that won't be necessary," the inspector said.

"He doesn't understand the language well enough," she said.

Alfredo stepped in here. "But I can do it on my own. Penelope, you have not to worry. All will be well."

I had never heard him address her so sweetly before. She looked rather more frantic than I thought she should. Once again I wondered what was going on between the two of them.

When the door closed behind them, Penelope slumped to the wall. I put a hand on her shoulder and said, "Let's go sit down. Did you sleep well last night? You look a little peaky."

She let me lead her down the hall, and then she burst into a rant. "Just because he's a foreigner, they think he did it. That's so like the police. Alfredo is a good man, and he didn't even want Sally's money or anything. He told me."

"I believe you," I said, steering her to a seat. "So you're sure he wouldn't have killed Sally?"

"Not in a million years. He didn't want to hurt her. You might not know this, but he was trying to break it off with her."

"And how do you know this?" I asked.

"Well, he had to tell someone."

"Why was he breaking it off?" I wanted to hear how Alfredo had explained himself to Penelope.

She dropped her head and fussed with a button on her blouse. "He said he didn't feel the same way anymore."

"Was there someone else?" I asked, prying a little more.

"I think there was," she said with a half smile on her lips.

∾

TWENTY-FIVE

Ring-a-Ding-Ding

The police had taken down the crime scene tape and said we could go back into the library. Caldwell went off to run some errands, and I decided I would try to put the books back in some semblance of order. I wanted to do it when he wasn't around, as I was worried there would be damage to some of the books. I wanted to repair what I could before he saw them.

But when I walked up the stairs, I noticed the door to the library was open, and when I looked in I saw a man standing in the middle of the floor, slowly turning around, completely absorbed in perusing all the books. It was

Bruce, and I knew Caldwell didn't want him in there by himself.

"Hello there," I said in a friendly voice. "Can I be of help?"

He startled, as he should, and said, "The door was open, or rather, not locked, and Caldwell had been promising me a look."

"I know, and you will have a look, but not until he's here to help you. I'm merely a librarian, not a full-fledged collector like you two."

"Yes, I can see by his books that he knows quality when he finds it. This is quite a wonderful collection."

"I'm glad you approve," I said, ever so snarkily.

I could see his hands shake slightly as he gestured toward the stacks of books, so impatient was he to handle them.

"What books are you most interested in?" I asked, knowing full well that I could be in for a torrent of a list, having experienced it with other collectors.

"I try to keep myself open to all possibilities. When one starts collecting books, one never knows what one might find. A well-made first edition is always worth looking at."

I was surprised at his admission. "But surely you must have some areas you specialize in?"

"Oh, yes. I love books printed by small presses in the early twentieth century, like the Hogarth Press, for example.

Such wonderful, thoughtful books. And so few were produced."

"So you like Virginia Woolf?" I asked.

"I love her books, not that I've read them. I just admire what beautiful objects they are. And worth quite a lot of money, especially in FN."

I knew FN stood for fine condition, the penultimate designation for a collectible book.

"And then I adore children's books," he went on.

"I'm not sure about any Hogarth Press books, but I know Caldwell has a decent collection of children's books."

"Yes." Bruce turned his head longingly to the bookcase that housed most of them. "I'd love to have a look."

I had to be firm. "I can't allow that without Caldwell. They are, after all, his books, and I don't have any idea which ones he's even willing to sell."

Bruce's shoulders sagged. "When will he be here?"

"Soon, I hope. But I'm not sure when he'll be ready to show the books. He seems to want to wait until we have a proper store."

"I understand," Bruce said, and walked out of the room.

But I wasn't convinced he did.

The books had all been put back on the shelves by the police but completely helter-skelter. No sense of any order—not by size, not by color, not by author's name or title or by topic. I suppose book organization is just not in their job descriptions.

As I stood before these scrambled shelves I realized it was making me a little nauseous to look at them. Almost as if I didn't know where to start. A sense of hopelessness came over me like a dark fog.

Things need to be in their proper place. Just as each book has one spot to be in the Dewey decimal system, so it is with a crime. There is a victim and there is a murderer. There is the truth of what happened. That's the way it is. I should be able to line up everyone—Alfredo, Brenda, Bruce, Caldwell, Karen, Penelope, Sally—and put them where they belong.

There was a second reason I was tackling the books. I had a sense that if I could know why Sally was in the library it might help me figure out who had killed her and why.

I remembered the toppled bookcase well. It was the one I had just finished organizing when Sally had rung the front doorbell at the very beginning of this whole disastrous affair.

The top three shelves contained history books, specifically English history. I slowly moved through the ages, putting books about early England on the top shelf. I had to stop and browse through a book on Ethelred, the not-ready king of Britain from around A.D. 1000. He tried to save the country from the Danes by paying them off. He gave them so much money that they say it is easier to find an old English coin in Scandinavia than in the British Isles.

After an hour's work, I had made my way down to present-day England and had to resist peeking into many of the books. I promised myself that I would read the books on the abdication of Edward VIII very soon. People had so many different opinions on his wife, the previously married Wallis Simpson. Why are nasty people so much more interesting than good ones?

Finally I found the book I had been looking for, the one I thought just might be Sally's because I was sure that it wasn't Caldwell's. I pulled it off the shelf where it had been tucked in between some history book and a book on gardening: a biography of Princess Diana called *The Diana Chronicles*. It was written by Tina Brown, the former editor of the extremely gossipy magazine *Tatler*. I was sure it was juicy as all get-out and equally sure that Caldwell would never have read it.

Opening it up to the copyright page, I saw the book wasn't even a first edition. This made me more sure that it was one of Sally's few books. In fact, it could have been the book Sally was looking for the night she died.

I paged through it, stopping to look at the pictures. Diana on horseback, Diana with long hair, Diana at her wedding, her sons. Diana always impressed me, with her short, thick haircut, as a very handsome young woman. But I felt like there was almost a prince-like quality about her.

What could there be about this book that would make Sally get up in the middle of the night to look for it?

Just as I was about to put the book where it belonged on the shelf, I noticed it didn't close as it should. When I turned to the very back of the book, I saw that there was a hole cut out in the middle of the pages, and in the hole was a tiny envelope taped shut.

I carefully unsealed it and dumped the contents into my hand.

A ring.

A Victorian, quite an exuberant ring with jewels galore, mostly diamonds, I thought, and one rather large green stone in the middle.

The size made me think it could have been some kind of cocktail ring, not an everyday ring.

I was quite sure I had found the ring that Sally and Penelope had fought over and that Sally was said to have stolen from her sister.

This had to be what Sally was looking for.

And I was probably the reason she couldn't find it.

That very day I had rearranged the books and put that particular book way up at the top of a different bookcase than where it had been, in the very bookcase that had fallen over on her.

I hated to think it but, if the book had been where she had left it, Sally might still be alive.

TWENTY-SIX

A Killing

I tried the ring on. It was too big for my ring finger but came close to fitting my middle finger. Sally and Penelope were both bigger women than me, and their hands were certainly larger too. I closed the door of the library and locked it, then walked down the hall toward Penelope's room.

Before I knocked on her door, I gathered myself together. What did I want to learn?

I turned the ring around so the stones faced my palm and, seeing only the plain gold band, Penelope wouldn't recognize it. I wanted to learn how she felt about her sister, Sally, and what the ring had meant to her before she realized what I already knew. When I looked at the whole blasted situation head-on, I had to ask myself whether Penelope could have killed her sister.

I hoped not. I had come to like Penelope for her quiet, quirky ways. And the fact that she wasn't Sally.

I knocked.

Sheets rustled inside the room.

I knocked again.

"Yes?" Penelope's voice quavered.

"May I come in? It's Karen," I announced.

"Of course. Give me a moment." I heard the bed creak, footsteps crossing the room, then water running. Had I caught her sleeping?

Suddenly the door opened and Penelope stood before me: her face wiped clear of makeup, a white T-shirt on and loose jeans, her hair pulled back in a messy ponytail. She looked younger and more vulnerable than usual.

"I'm sorry about all this," I found myself saying, although I wasn't sure what I was sorry about since none of it was my fault.

"Yes." She nodded and ushered me into her room.

The bed looked a scramble, almost as if more than one person had been sleeping in it. Penelope ushered me to a small table with two chairs that was sitting by the window. We both took a seat.

She set her chin in her hands. "Yes," she said again, "first

Sally dead, then Caldwell suspected of her death, and now Alfredo taken away by the police. It's just too much."

"Are you sure Alfredo had nothing to do with what happened to Sally? No reason to want her dead?"

Without hesitation, she responded, "Very sure."

I asked, "Why?"

She lifted her hands up and waved them around as if trying to encompass a large thought. "Because he just couldn't. Alfredo doesn't have enough gumption to kill someone. He's just too easygoing and sweet."

I had to agree with her.

"Could you?" I asked.

"Yes," she admitted after a moment. "I'm surprised to say it, but I think I could kill someone. I've given it some thought—you know how you do when you're faced with one of these life-changing situations—and I've come to see that, in the right circumstances, I could kill someone."

"Did you?"

She looked up at me and then covered her mouth as she laughed. "Sally? No, I wouldn't bother."

"Even if she took something that was near and dear to you?" I asked, feeling the ring in the palm of my hand.

"Which she did often when we were young." Penelope stopped to think, then said, "No, I was used to it. Although I have to wonder how she would have felt if I did it back to her."

I slid the ring around on my finger and then held my hand out to her. "Is this yours?"

She grabbed my hand with both of hers. "Oh my lord. My ring! Where did you find it?"

"In a book."

"A book? What do you mean?"

"I found it tucked into a book in the library. Sally must have put it there for safekeeping."

Penelope burst out, "I knew she had taken it. She denied it up and down, but I always knew."

"Why would she take it and then leave it behind in the library when she left Caldwell?" I asked.

"Oh, I think she just didn't want me to have it. That was so Sally. If she knew I liked something, she would do something to ruin it."

I slipped the ring off my finger, handed it to Penelope, and then watched her slide it on the ring finger of her right hand. On my hand it had looked gaudy, but somehow on her hand it looked elegant, even regal.

"Thank you so much for finding it. I can't tell you what it means to me. Maybe some things are going to turn out all right after all."

"You're welcome." I got up to leave. "Are you going to be okay?"

"Yes, thanks. It was just so hard watching the police take Alfredo away. I felt so powerless."

"Yes, I know what you mean. What is going on between you two?"

She looked down at her ring, held it out to see it better, then said, "Something."

"You know when you said that you could kill someone— would you have killed someone for that ring?"

Penelope kept admiring the ring as she held her arm out straight, turning it this way and that. "No, not for the ring."

"Alfredo?" I asked.

She clasped her hand around the ring. "For him, I might."

∽◇∾

TWENTY-SEVEN

Hopping Down the Bunny Trail

"Things have really gotten bollixed up," Caldwell said as we sat down to eat dinner in the kitchen, where we could be away from the guests. All that was on the table was one big casserole of Yorkshire hotpot.

I didn't think it would do to argue with him about how bollixed up things were. "I know," I said as I served both of us the dish.

He didn't say anything. I stabbed a fork into a pile of overcooked potatoes with bits of bacon in them. I could tell how off Caldwell was feeling, because his cooking was rapidly deteriorating.

"How are we to decide what we want to do? How am I to convince you to stay here in England and start our new venture when I don't even completely own my major asset?" he asked.

"That's not so important," I said. "That wasn't really what I've been trying to figure out."

"Explain to me again your thoughts," he said, reaching out and rubbing my hand with his thumb. "Do I stand a chance with you?"

"More than a chance. It's hardly about you at all. You're perfect, or as close to perfect as one can expect in this imperfect world."

At that he tweaked my nose.

I continued, "I'm trying to see if I can give up my life back home, my work as a librarian, my friends, my house, my books, my walks, my everything . . . to come and live with you in this world that I don't completely understand and in which people get killed far too often for my taste."

"Okay, now we're getting someplace. First off, I need you as a librarian. You will help me order my books, organize my life. In my eyes, you will always be the librarian of our books. Second, your books will come with you, I hope, to commingle with mine. Third, as they say, *mi casa es su casa*. And I hope your friends will come often to visit and that you will find new friends and new walks to make your life full and complete. And then there's me."

"Yes, the most potent argument of all—to live with a man who loves books and who loves me."

"Nearly as much as books," he murmured.

"I would be a fool not to grab you while I can," I said, pulling away to look at Caldwell.

"And no one would ever be caught dead calling you that," he said emphatically, then heard what he had said and apologized. "Sorry about the dead part."

"That is the part that worries me now. I can hardly think of all the rest of it until we have that part figured out. What if they take you away again? What if it was Alfredo? What if they think it's me?"

"You? Why would they think you did it?"

"Because of you."

"Oh, now this is getting ridiculous," he said.

"You don't think I have it in me to be a jealous, conniving woman who would slay anything in the way of getting her man?"

"Well, hardly conniving. The rest of it, perhaps."

"Caldwell, we must resolve what happened to Sally."

"And we will."

"I forgot to tell you that Bruce went into the library this morning. I found him in there snooping around."

It was as if I had thrown a glass of ice water in his face. Caldwell gulped, went white, and then stood up, shaking his head. "He was in the library?" he asked. "Alone? By himself?"

"Yes, but I don't think he had time to do anything. I

asked him what he wanted—which was to buy books from you. I explained to him that you weren't ready to sell and then sent him on his way."

"I must go and check on my books."

"I locked the room. I'm sure that everything is fine."

"But I haven't told you about something."

"The thing that you haven't told me about yet?" I asked. "The surprise that you've been keeping from me?"

"Yes, that thing. Well, I did want it to be a surprise, at the right moment, but I think you need to know now, because of how valuable it is and all that."

"Yes, I'm ready."

"But first I have to go and check the library." He dropped his napkin on the floor and bolted out of the room.

I followed behind him, at a slower pace. I caught up with him as he was fumbling with the key to unlock the door.

"Please let it still be there," he said as he pushed the door open.

Caldwell strode over to the Edwardian rolltop desk and unlocked the top to reveal a set of drawers and pigeonholes. Underneath one of the drawers, he pulled out a second small, secret drawer. From there, he took out a carefully wrapped rectangular object that I had no doubt was a book. Reverently, he placed it on the desktop.

Then he pointed to me. "Please unwrap it."

I knew this was an honor that he was bestowing on me.

I ever so carefully undid the tissue paper, which I was sure was archival, and stared at the cover of the book that was revealed: *The Tale of Peter Rabbit* by Beatrix Potter.

The cover was gray with an inset picture of Peter Rabbit in a blue coat running away. It had been published by F. Warne and Company, if I remembered correctly, in 1902.

"Not a first edition?" I gasped.

He only nodded.

"But it's worth a lot of money," I said.

He nodded again.

"Where did you find it?" I asked.

"At an estate sale. I got there late, and the woman in charge had just opened up the children's playroom in the attic. It was at the bottom of a pile of books. I couldn't believe it. I paid ten pounds for it. Ten pounds."

"But it's worth?" I couldn't even guess. I just knew it was one of the most valuable children's books.

"Five thousand times that."

"Oh my."

"Yes." Caldwell touched the cover gently with his finger. "And it's definitely VG if not FN."

"Yes, I can see that. And you were worried that Bruce might have found it. But how would he know about it?"

"I've been dumb," Caldwell said.

"How so?"

"I couldn't keep it to myself. I just had to tell someone

the news. I wanted to surprise you when you were here. So I e-mailed a friend, who happens to also be a collector. All I can guess is he spread the word. Bruce called a day or two later, nosing around. And now he's here."

"Has he asked you about the book?"

"No, he hasn't. Not directly. But I can smell it on him— book lust. Very distinctive. He goes out every day, but then he comes back and sniffs around here. Wants to talk about children's books. I can tell he wants it."

"Might you sell it to him?" I asked.

"I might. But not yet. I'm so enjoying having it. It's like looking for the Holy Grail and then you find it next to the rubbish bin one night. At first you can't believe it, then you start to believe it, then you are convinced of it. I'm not quite to the convinced part. I need to know that I have done this before I even think of letting the book go."

"To what end do you think he would go to get his hands on this book?"

"Hard to say. But I've heard stories of books that are found, then follows mysterious deaths and the books are never seen again."

"But surely not for Beatrix Potter?"

"One of the most valuable books in England."

I looked at the cover again, not even daring to open the pages. A little bunny rabbit hopping away. Who would have thought?

TWENTY-EIGHT

A Night Off

I was able to persuade Caldwell to put the bunny book back in its safe hiding place and to consider getting a safety deposit box in his bank the next day. He double-checked the lock on the library door as we stood in the hallway.

"You go on to bed," he said. "I'm just going to go down and finish the dishes and set things up for breakfast."

I knew he had his rituals about how everything must be left in the kitchen, so I did as he asked. But when I got into our bedroom, I sank onto the floor and couldn't quite bring myself to do all the things I had to do to get ready for bed. Sometimes brushing and flossing just seemed like too much work. I felt both stirred up and exhausted.

I dug in my pocket, pulled out my cell phone, and called Rosie. She sniffled when she picked up the phone, even before she said hello.

"Rosie?" I asked. "What's wrong?"

"Richard," she said.

"Is he sick? Has he been hurt? What's happened?"

"He thinks we're spending too much time together."

I almost laughed, but resisted. Rosie, who had always been the one to scamper away if ever a relationship got too serious, was now having this same reaction thrown back at her. "Does he want to see you less?"

"I'm not sure what he wants, but he said we should take a night off."

"Tonight?"

"Yes, and I miss him already and I'm not even done with work."

I didn't want to downplay what she was feeling, but I also wanted her to see that Richard hadn't made such an unfair request.

"What are you going to do with yourself tonight?" I asked.

"I don't know."

"What have you not done since you've started seeing Richard, that you miss doing? Something fun."

"I've been eating less. I suppose I could go on a Häagen-Dazs binge."

"Might do," I said. Rosie was maybe twenty pounds over-weight but had never seemed to worry about it before. Richard was tall and thin. I hoped he wasn't telling her she weighed too much. That would bode bad. "What about something more outgoing? A friend you haven't seen? A long walk?"

"Maybe I should get a puppy."

"Don't go getting drastic on me."

"I wish you and I could do something together. I miss you. Maybe I should come over to London."

I split in two—half of me wanted Rosie to jump on the next plane and come and witness what might become my new life, one I hoped she would be part of; the other half didn't want her to have to step into the craziness that was going on at the B and B. "Maybe wait a week or two. It's pretty confusing here right now. Also, Nancy would lose her mind if you left."

"Maybe Richard would miss me. That would be good, right?"

"I'm sure he would miss you."

"Have you figured out how that woman was killed?"

"Well, we've always known she was killed by too many books, but not how they happened to fall over on top of her, which the police have determined could not have been an accident."

"And you don't know who did it?"

I closed the door, not wanting Caldwell to come in while

I was going over the list of suspects. I knew he didn't want me messing around with this murder.

"Well, I think it has to be one of four people. That's not including Caldwell, because there's no way he could have done it."

"Maybe he did it for you?" Rosie suggested.

"What?" I squawked.

"You know, so you could go ahead with your plans."

"Rosie, you don't know him. He's a strong, thoughtful man, but gentle as can be. Plus, we can go ahead with our plans anyway. If that's what we decide to do."

"Okay, so who are the four suspects?"

"The two prime suspects are Penelope, the sister, and Alfredo, the lover."

"Oh, I like that. They do sound good."

"Yes, but I don't think either of them did it. I think they've got something going, and somehow I just don't see how that would lead them to murder her. Unless she had something on one of them that she threatened to tell the other."

"Could be," Rosie said.

"Then there are the less-than-prime suspects: Bruce and Brenda. Bruce is a book collector extraordinaire, and Brenda is Caldwell's helper around here. But Bruce didn't even know Sally, and Brenda adored her. I'm close to ruling them out."

Rosie gurgle-laughed. "It sounds to me like you're ruling everyone out."

I sighed. "I guess I am. But it has to be one of them. I feel like there's something I'm missing."

"I would like to point out to you that Caldwell had the best reasons for wanting Sally out of the way. One, he didn't like her. Two, she deserted him. Three, she was threatening him with taking away part of the B and B. Four, revenge. Plus, maybe he thought he would lose you."

"Just because Richard is asking for a night off doesn't mean you can take it out on Caldwell."

"Think about it."

So I did for a moment. Listening to Rosie's list of reasons for murder, I thought of one that might apply to Alfredo. What if there was something going on between Alfredo and Penelope, and Sally was standing in the way?

"You've given me an idea. Thanks," I said.

"And somehow you've made me feel better," she said.

"Yes, my advice is enjoy your one night away from your guy. And I'll try to figure out what's happened here."

"I think I'll go shopping tonight."

"That's a good idea," I said.

"Call me when you've figured the murder out."

"I will, no matter what time it is." After I hung up the phone, I stayed sitting on the floor. I needed to do some checking into Alfredo. Who was he? What did we really know about him?

∽⌒⌒⌒∽

TWENTY-NINE

Throes of Passion

Questions whirled around my mind like a merry-go-round on steroids that night, not allowing me to sleep very well. Caldwell was snoring gently beside me. The sound was often a lovely white-noise machine for me, but that night it didn't seem to be working. Every hour I would peek my eyes open and check the clock. Finally around three in the morning I caved in, my mind went blank, and I fell into a dreamless sleep.

The house was quiet and empty when I awoke at nine. Caldwell had left a pot of tea, which had stayed mildly warm under a tea cozy. He had also left me a note that read: "I've gone off on a wild-goose chase. More later when I return.

Mary Lou Kirwin

Back for lunch. Penelope went to her mom's, Alfredo went off on some mysterious errand. I love you true. C."

I couldn't help pressing the note to my chest. He did love me true, and I loved him too. That was enough for right now.

After making some toast, I went and sat in the love seat and looked at the garden. Sally's garden. Sally. She continued to be the problem. But I had resolved to solve it, and then I would decide how to live my life.

Alfredo would be a good person to start on. I would find out everything I could about him. I hurriedly ate my toast and then ran upstairs to dress. This felt like a workday, so I put on a plain white blouse and a clean pair of jeans. I laced on my tennis shoes and rolled up my sleeves. Time to get things solved.

Then I checked the house out—no one was about. Brenda wasn't working, so even she was gone. I might never have another chance like this. I retrieved the keys to the rooms from the cupboard in the kitchen.

In front of Alfredo's door, I paused for a moment. If he returned while I was in his room, I could just say I was changing the towels. To cover my alibi, I grabbed some towels out of the linen closet.

I opened the door and walked in. I shut the door gently and stood, letting my heart quiet and my eyes circle the room. The bed hadn't been properly dressed yet, but some attempt had been made to pull the sheets and blankets up. A book lay facedown on the bedside table. A suitcase was open with clothes strewing out of it. When I opened the closet, I saw women's clothing. Sally's. She had taken over the whole closet. Didn't surprise me.

The outfit Sally had been wearing the first day she had come to the B and B was hanging right in front of me, slightly wrinkled looking. My hands slipped into the pockets, and in one I found a piece of paper, blocky handwriting on it: "Don't worry. I'll take care of her."

I carefully folded the note and put it in my pocket. The handwriting didn't look familiar. Who would take care of whom?

The suitcase was the next object I searched. In a side pocket I found a copy of Sally's last will and testament. It was dated the day before Alfredo and Sally had come to the B and B. In it Alfredo was designated as the heir. I wondered if he had known about it before they arrived. He had acted surprised when he received the news of his inheritance, but maybe it had been just an act.

I needed to talk to Sally's lawyer. I wrote down his name, William Pendergast, and put the will back where I had found it.

I heard voices in the hall coming toward the room.

Suddenly the idea of pretending to change the towels seemed unbelievable. Plus, there were two voices, and they were coming from right outside the door—Penelope and Alfredo.

I heard Alfredo say, "Come, my darling. We have waited long enough. There's no one here."

The key was rattling in the lock.

Without thinking I dropped to my knees and slid under the bed, towels still in my arms.

From my crunched position, I could see the bottom of the door swing open and two pairs of shoes walk in. One was a very fine pair of Italian men's shoes, and the other was simple black pumps. The four shoes walked to the end of the bed, and then two bodies fell onto the mattress.

My heart sank. What had I done?

Alfredo was whispering a stream of lovely and passionate phrases, and Penelope was merely sighing back, "Yes, yes, yes."

I was thinking, *No, no, no.*

As they moved around, the bed sank on top of me, making the small space I had squeezed into even tighter. I felt like I couldn't breathe. I wondered if there was any way I could sneak out of the room while they were in the throes of passion.

I squirmed around until I was facing the bottom of the bed, not far from the door. I thought I'd wait until I saw clothes being flung to the floor. Count to ten and then wriggle out and, staying low, open the door just wide enough to slide out. It might work. But probably not.

Maybe it would have worked, but no clothes were flung. Then one pair of shoes with feet still in them hit the floor. "Tell me why you don't think the will is legal," I heard Penelope say.

"Not now, my pastry shell. There will be time for all of that later. But now I just want to put my nose in your bosom," Alfredo said.

His shoes came down next to hers. The two of them were standing just inches from my nose. Four shoes that I could almost lick if I wanted to. I could see that Penelope had a run in her hose. Alfredo's socks were a muted stripe, probably silk, and very elegant. The guy knew how to dress, I'd give him that.

Again, they were holding on to each other, kissing and clearly blocking my way out of the room.

Just when I thought I could stand it no longer, a dear voice called from down the hall. "Alfredo, may I speak to you for a moment?"

Penelope hissed, "It's Caldwell. He mustn't see us together. I think he already suspects something."

I certainly suspected something. But I wasn't exactly sure what. How long had they been an item? I wondered. Long enough to be a problem for Sally? Long enough for one or both of them to want to get rid of her? But why? It didn't exactly make sense. How would her death serve them?

"It's okay now. Everything will turn out as we have wanted," Alfredo said. "You will see."

"I hope so," Penelope said. "But we need to be careful. I think you should go out and talk to him. Take him downstairs and then I can get out of the room."

"Oh, but I have such great desires for you."

"I have for you too, my darling. But we will have our time. Soon." She moved him toward the door.

"Tonight," he said.

"We'll see," she said as she shoved him out the door. It closed, and she leaned up against it, sighing.

I wiggled back to make sure I was out of sight. She came and sat on the edge of the bed right over me. A hand appeared and picked at the run in her stockings.

I heard footsteps going down the stairs, and the bed lifted as Penelope stood up. After waiting at the door for a moment, she carefully opened it and left the room.

I waited another minute after I heard her bedroom door shut, then slithered out from under the bed and brushed myself off. I grabbed the towels I had carried into the room and opened the door.

I had only taken two steps into the hallway when Penelope's door swung open. "Karen," she said. "I didn't know you were here."

"Oh, I was doing some laundry," I said, and offered her the towels. "Do you need some clean ones?"

"No, thank you," she said, strode past me to the stairs, and descended.

I put my head in the towels, aswirl with what I had learned—Penelope and Alfredo were definitely a couple.

❧

THIRTY

King for a Day

"Can you do something for me?" I asked Caldwell when Alfredo and Penelope finally left for dinner, claiming they needed to go over the details of the will. I knew better. And so did Caldwell, as I had filled him in on some of what I had heard them talk about.

"Of course, but wait a minute. How did you learn that these two were together? Did you see them?"

We were in the kitchen, sitting at the table and drinking the end of a bottle of very nice red wine.

"Sort of," I said, embarrassed to tell him.

"Yes?"

"It has to do with what I'd like you to do."

"How so?"

"Well, I was trying to check on Alfredo. So I let myself into his room."

"Really?" Caldwell asked, trying to sound stern, but I could see he was enjoying this.

"Yes, and then they both came in."

"And where were you?"

This was the part that was hard to admit. "I slipped under the bed."

"Under the bed?"

"Yes, and things started to get a little hot and heavy, but then Penelope backed out."

Caldwell didn't say anything for a moment, taking in what I had told him. Finally he said with a laugh, "You might have found out more about Alfredo than you cared to know."

"Yes," I admitted weakly.

Caldwell poured the last few drops into my glass, toasted me, and said, "So what would you like me to do?"

"Do some checking up on Alfredo, please."

"Why?"

"I think we should know who he is, not who he says he is. There's something that isn't right there."

"You don't honestly think he killed Sally, do you?"

"You know it's a very strong possibility that no one intended to kill Sally. Maybe they just wanted to frighten her.

I could see Alfredo doing that. We know now that he was planning on dumping her for her sister."

"Karen, remember the state they were in that night. Fairly inebriated. How could he have had the wherewithal to conceive a plan like that, let alone carry it out?"

"It sounded like he was gone in his cups—but who knows how drunk he actually was. He might have been faking it."

"You have a very devious mind. Remind me never to get on the wrong side of you."

"I don't think you could do that."

We kissed. But then I continued. "Remember that Sally had said he was of the House of Savoy. Well, that's like claiming he's related to the king of Italy. I don't know much about the family, but it would be interesting to see if he really is any relation to them."

"He could be a fraud and still not have killed Sally."

"Oh, I know, but I'm curious." I cuddled up to him. "And you are such a whiz on the computer."

"I've always wanted to be a whiz," Caldwell said, giving me his darling half smile.

"I'll even do the dishes."

"'Bout time you carried your weight around here," he said as he left me in the kitchen.

I had just wiped down the counters when he came back in the room and said excitedly, "Come and see what I have discovered."

Caldwell kept his laptop in his bedroom, set under the front windows overlooking the street, on a small oak desk. He pulled a chair up for me, and first he showed me one picture of an old man in a dark suit. The caption underneath read: "Alfredo Remulado von Savoy." However, the man was obviously not our Alfredo.

"Could be his father," I said.

"Yes, perhaps. But I have something else to show you."

He went to a travel website called Viva Italia! Then he clicked on a button that said "Tours." A picture came up that showed a tall and handsome man standing in front of a lovely villa. The man had a big, toothy smile and was flourishing one hand as if inviting all to come in.

The man was our Alfredo.

But the caption underneath read: "Giuseppe Molto, tour guide extraordinaire, will show you around the magnificent Villa Pelouza, where you may sample the fine wines and cheeses of the region."

"Do you think Sally knew about this?" I asked.

"She probably did. Sally loved playacting. She would have fallen right into his role-playing."

"What about Penelope?"

Caldwell shrugged. "It's hard to know what went on when Penelope went down to visit. Maybe Sally and Alfredo fooled her the whole time she was there."

"But to what end?"

"Just for the fun of it."

"What do you think Penelope would do if she found out? Would she have blamed Sally?"

Caldwell thought for a moment. "I don't think such a stunt would have caused her to want to hurt her sister—but years of such things might have. Sally was not always very nice to Penelope, often putting her down and teasing her. I actually think Sally was fond of Penelope, but I'm not sure her younger sister ever really knew it."

"So maybe this charade was the straw that ended up breaking Sally's back instead of Penelope's."

Caldwell said, "Maybe."

◇◇◇

THIRTY-ONE

Rolling, Rolling

I heard Caldwell get out of bed to start breakfast for the guests, but I couldn't quite rouse myself. I'm not sure how much longer I slept, but when I woke up the sun was definitely shining, and I could hear the sound of people talking downstairs. Time to rise and shine, as my father would say.

Caldwell had emptied out two drawers for me in his dresser, but as I scrounged in them I saw that it was getting to be time to do a load or two of wash. I was running out of outfits to wear. I put on a long-sleeved shirt and a pair of brown corduroy pants. I threw water on my face, brushed my teeth, and took a comb to my hair. It would have to be good enough.

I wasn't sure what was on our agenda today: finish straightening up the library, read the paper, maybe go book shopping, which we had hardly done since I arrived. Such an outing would be a treat for Caldwell and me, and lord knows we needed a treat. Oh, and find out who had pushed the bookcase over on Sally. Priority number one.

Still trying to wake up, I started down the stairs. The voices from the garden room grew louder. I could hear Alfredo's (or Giuseppe's) booming voice above all the rest. I could see how he would make a good tour guide.

Halfway down the stairs, I took a step and my foot hit something round. I went flying.

Thank goodness I remembered the crash course I had taken on jumping out of an airplane. For a couple of weeks, I had dated a paratrooper who wanted to take me skydiving. I never went. I was so thankful we broke up before the scheduled flight. But I still remembered the lessons I had taken in preparation for it—on how to land safely on the ground from a very high fall.

So as I was flying through the air, I managed to tuck and turn on my side. I landed on the carpet at the bottom of the stairs with a big thump. The side of my back and my hip took the force of the landing. Both areas were fairly well padded, but I still had the breath knocked out of me.

Before I could move or speak, or even breathe, I was surrounded by everyone in the house: Bruce, Alfredo, Penelope,

Brenda, and, of course, Caldwell. Their faces peered down at me like I was a mouse in a maze. I felt stunned.

Caldwell knelt beside me and held my shoulders. "Don't move," he said. "We need to make sure you haven't broken anything."

I gasped for air. "Yes," I wheezed.

His hands felt along my legs and then my arms and my neck. "Where does it hurt? Can you move everything?"

"Yes, I think so." I whistled a word at a time, trying to reassure him while I was not so sure of my okayness. "Let me catch my breath."

"Give her some room," he said to everyone who was crowding over me. They all stepped back, and I felt like I could breathe again.

Slowly I sat up. The room didn't spin, nothing felt broken, but I knew I was going to have one heck of a bruise on my hip.

"What happened?" Caldwell asked me.

"I stepped on something on the stairs," I said.

Everyone looked behind me and then shook their heads. I turned my head around and saw what they had seen. Nothing. There was nothing on the stairs, yet I could completely remember the feeling of a rounded thing under my foot.

"There was something there," I said. "I'm sure of it."

"You probably caught your toe," Penelope said.

"Just so long as you're all right," Bruce joined in.

"I cleaned the stairs yesterday," Brenda said. "So they might have been a bit slippy."

"What do you think it was?" Caldwell asked.

At least he believed me.

"Oh, silly me. You're all probably right," I said, trying my best to sound lighthearted about my slip.

I knew I hadn't caught my toe or slipped on the stairs. The rounded object had been under the ball of my foot. But I decided not to argue. I would act as if everything was okay. If someone had put something on the stairs, maybe it was better not to let them know I was onto them.

Caldwell helped me up and, while my hip ached, nothing seemed to be broken or even sprained.

But I would find out who had put something on the stairs for me to trip over. I knew it had not been an accident.

THIRTY-TWO

Shopping as Antidote

After all the guests had cleared out for the morning, I checked around the stairs, looking for something that I might have tripped over. The hall was clean and empty, but the kitchen was right next to the stairs. Whoever had done it might have stashed the implement there. But when I started to look, Caldwell came in and asked me what I was doing. I didn't want to tell him there. I felt like someone might overhear us and I wanted to be cautious.

"You're limping a bit," he said.

"I'm fine," I assured him.

"Sit down. I'll make you some tea."

When Caldwell and I were sitting down for a "cuppa" on our own—actually, he was doing the dishes and I was sitting with my feet up, resting from my fall—I said, "Let's go look at some old books in a store you haven't shown me yet. Remember your long list of shops we were planning on visiting—to get ideas and maybe some books?"

He turned around so fast, he sprayed the kitchen with water from his hands. "Really?" he asked. "Do you think you're up to it?"

I stood up, trying not to show how much my hip ached, brushed myself off, and said, "Absolutely good to go."

"That would be lovely," he said.

I loved how men in England could say *lovely* and not sound like a prissy lady. I couldn't imagine an American male ever saying the word *lovely*, even to his girlfriend, even when she was lovely.

"You're sure?" he asked again. "I've been wanting to show you this new smallish shop that I've discovered. It's walking distance away. Could you manage a walk, do you think?"

"I think a nice, easy walk with books at the end would be just what the doctor ordered," I said.

"What a smart doctor," Caldwell said, and wiped his hands on a towel. "I can be ready to go in a sec."

"Me too," I said. When he turned back to put the dishes away, I hobbled out of the kitchen. As I walked I noticed that my hip eased up and my back didn't hurt so much. Some movement would be good for me.

It was a perfect English day: brisk enough for a coat, but not so cold you needed a hat; a scattering of clouds in the sky, but nothing ominous. Caldwell and I started off. He took my arm, and we walked slowly down the streets. I felt so at home with him by my side.

As much as I hated to ruin our contentedness, I had to tell him of my concern. "You know when I fell . . ."

"Yes, it was awful," he said as if I needed reassurance.

"Yes, whatever. But what I'm trying to tell you is I'm sure I stepped on something."

He nodded. "I don't doubt it. I've never seen you be clumsy or trip. On the contrary, you are exceptionally stable."

"Well, be that as it may, I felt something under my foot and it was round—like a can or a rolling pin."

"Rolling pin?" he asked, his eyebrows shooting up to the middle of his forehead. "Are you sure?"

"Yes, why?"

"When I was putting the dishes away this morning, I went to put the silver in the drawer and found the rolling pin in there. Not where it belongs. But it is the closest drawer to the door."

"That is interesting. Who had the opportunity to put it on the stairs and then replace it in the kitchen?"

Caldwell stopped walking, and so I stopped too. He

thought, then shook his head. "I'm afraid everyone. Except me. I was totally focused on you, so I wasn't watching what anyone else was doing."

"And the kitchen is so close to the stairs it wouldn't have been hard for anyone to put the rolling pin back."

"It might have been an accident. Both your fall and that the rolling pin was in the wrong drawer," Caldwell said, and I could tell he was trying to convince himself of this possibility because the alternative was so unpleasant. We started walking again, holding hands.

"Yes," I said. "But I rather doubt it."

He sighed. "Why would anyone want to hurt you? You might have been . . ." Again, he stopped as he thought of what might have happened. "Why, Karen, you might have been killed."

"Yes, I know."

"What is going on?"

"Someone is very angry about something."

"But what do you have to do with that?" he asked.

"Maybe they don't like it that I'm nosing around. Maybe they think if I was put out of action by a fall, you would end up taking the blame for Sally's death and they would be safe."

"Yes, that must be it." He grabbed my arm even tighter than before and we continued walking.

"Or," I said, "maybe someone just doesn't like me."

~∞~

THIRTY-THREE

What Would HP Do?

The shop wasn't on Caldwell's list of the best booksellers in London, but it was small and quaint, and struck me as a good model for the shop we were thinking of starting. A sign that read FUDGEWINKLE'S FOLLY hung above the door and made me like it already.

When we walked in three things happened: a tinkling bell rang; a large, orange-colored cat, stretched out in a spot of sun, raised its head; and an older, thin man sitting behind a desk looked up from the book he was reading. All of which I took for good signs.

Also, my hip was feeling better. The walk and Caldwell's concern had more than improved my spirits.

"Good day," the thin man said.

We both answered that it was a good day. The thin man, I saw as we got closer, was not as old as I'd thought he might be. He just dressed old—wearing a bow tie and a ratty cardigan sweater. While his clothes spoke of someone in his eighties, his smooth face and dark hair said thirties.

I couldn't help myself. I had to ask. "Are you Fudgewinkle?"

The thin man smiled. "No, that's Fudgewinkle." He pointed at the cat, who was now in the process of cleaning an outstretched leg. "This, however," he said, moving an arm to encompass the shop, "is the folly."

"And a wonderful folly it is," said Caldwell, and he stepped forward to shake the thin man's hand. "Poppy, this is my friend, Karen Nash, from America. Karen, this is Poppy Stoneheart, bookseller extraordinaire." The thin man then shook my hand.

"Anything new come in that I might be interested in? You know my taste," Caldwell said.

"As in something I might tempt you with?" Poppy asked. "I had the extreme good fortune recently to buy up the entire library of an old estate—a marvelous collection although not in the best shape. I just finished putting the books where they belong, so you'll have to look around to find them."

I noticed that there were signs above most of the shelves

categorizing the books. Most helpful. I found the shelf of mysteries and decided I would start there. As I stood in front of the rows of books, reaching too far above my head, I felt like I was back with my own people: Josephine Tey, Dorothy Sayers, Ngaio Marsh, the older vanguard of British women mystery writers. I loved them dearly and was always on the lookout for a new addition to my library.

I had to remind myself that I should really be shopping for our store, and then caught myself as I thought the word *our*. After all, I hadn't yet made a decision on my involvement with said store. But I found it hard to think of Caldwell starting the store without me. I made note of that. Maybe I was closer to a decision than I knew. How odd to be surprised by oneself.

The books were shelved in very good order—simple, just alphabetical by author's name, but often, like with Agatha Christie, they were also alphabetical by title. This was a touch that made my librarian's heart sing.

Suddenly I saw a book I had never seen but only read about—*Ten Little Niggers* by Agatha Christie—the first British edition, published in 1939 by the Collins Crime Club.

When it came out in the United States the next year, the title, because it was so politically incorrect (even though that phrase hadn't been coined yet), was changed to *And Then There Were None*. The book became Christie's bestselling novel and the bestselling mystery of all time.

I wanted it. For me.

The price was six thousand dollars. Way out of my range. But probably worth it—the dust jacket was in very good condition, featuring ten small black men dancing on a disk with a hand coming down to pick one of them up.

As I held the book out in front of me, I foresaw a problem with buying books for the store—would I want them all for myself? I needed to learn how to shop for the general public, and that meant learning the prices on books and what was a deal, what we could make money on.

I made myself put the book back on the shelf and pulled down another of Agatha Christie's books, a lovely original edition of *Appointment with Death*.

I always loved the books of hers that included a scene where Hercule Poirot meets with all the suspects and, to the amazement of the police, explains how and why the murders were done. There was something about this clarity that so pleased my library mind—a place for everything and everything in its place.

I closed my eyes, held the book to my chest, and savored it. What a genius Agatha Christie was. She wrote book after book, murder after unusual murder, then solved each one with some nice neat little package of a treatise.

Then my thoughts shifted to our own possible murder case. How I would love to turn into Poirot, replete with mustache, and call the possible suspects—Penelope, Alfredo, Brenda, Bruce, and, yes, Caldwell and myself—to the garden room, where I would then explain how the books came to tumble down on Sally.

Maybe I could do it—if I knew the answers to a few more questions.

THIRTY-FOUR

࿇

A Little Cry

When we got home, Caldwell went upstairs to take a nap and I wandered toward the back room to page through my new books. Besides the Agatha Christie I had splurged on a Tey and a Marsh. I was just getting used to the idea that I could spend a little more money on books than I was used to. Again, bless the Flush Budget. Who would have thought so much good could come from a toilet?

I thought it very sweet that Caldwell was comfortable enough with me that he would take a nap if he needed one and not worry about me. The thought of him sleeping was in itself comforting.

When I walked into the garden room, I found two weeping women—Penelope and Brenda—already occupying it. Penelope was using a lovely linen handkerchief to wipe her tears away, while Brenda was using what looked to be a dustrag. I hoped it had not been used earlier for its original purpose.

"I'm sorry," I said as they looked up at me while wiping their faces.

"Oh, not to worry," Penelope said. "We're just having a little cry together. I can't believe Sally's gone. It's like this huge chunk of my life just vanished. Even though she could be difficult, she was my sister."

"And I didn't even get to talk to her," Brenda chimed in. "I've been waiting so long to see her again and now I never will. I had always hoped she'd come back and live here again. But it's all over. Mr. Caldwell is leaving and I'll be out in the streets. I wish I were dead."

With those words, both of them burst into tears again.

I sat down in the love seat next to Penelope, poured them each more tea. They'd need liquid to replenish what they were losing through their tears. I waited for the tears to subside.

Finally they blew their noses, snuffled back the end of the tears, and reached for their teas. Brenda, as was her habit, poured a good amount of milk into hers. They both stirred and blew and drank.

The English and their tea. They had made drinking it into as much a ceremony as had the Japanese.

I saw this as my chance to ask the two of them a few more questions that might solidify my thoughts on Sally's death. "Do either of you have any further ideas on how Sally died?"

Brenda said, "I know for a fact that Mr. Caldwell couldn't have done it. I'm pretty sure I heard him rattling around down in the kitchen right before I heard the loud thump of the books falling. If you ask me, I think it was an accident. I'm sure of it." She lowered her head and stared into her cup.

"The hook undone?"

Brenda shook her head, then in a voice with little assurance she said, "Circumstantial evidence. I might have undone the hook myself by accident when I was in there cleaning."

"I thought you didn't dust the books," I reminded her.

"Mostly I don't. But sometimes I can't resist, you know, if Caldwell hasn't been in there for a while."

"I certainly didn't do it," Penelope said, looking right at me, her eyes lightly rimmed with red. "I didn't even know there was a bookcase in front of that door. I'd never been in the library before."

"What about Alfredo?" I asked. "After all, he had the most to gain from her death after she changed the will."

Penelope jumped as if she'd been stuck by a pin. "No. He's rich. He wouldn't need the money."

"Are you sure?" I asked.

"Of course I'm sure. I stayed at his villa," she said.

"And you know it was his?" I asked.

Penelope's eyes widened for a moment, then she said, "What are you suggesting? Whose else would it be? He lived there and knew the history of it going way back to the Middle Ages."

"Neither point proves anything," I said.

"What's the matter with you?" Penelope asked. "Why do you keep poking around about this?"

"Because Caldwell might be found guilty of causing Sally's death. I won't let that happen."

"If anyone's to blame, it's you." Brenda stood and continued. "It's really all your fault. If you hadn't come along, we'd all have been fine. Sally would still be alive." She huffed out of the room.

"What's going on between you and Alfredo?" I asked Penelope. "I couldn't help noticing that you seem to have gotten awfully chummy since your sister's death. Are you lovers?"

Penelope slitted her eyes. "Don't you start anything about that. Alfredo and I were going to tell Sally. We got quite close when I visited them, and now, seeing each other again, we knew it was more than infatuation. We were planning on telling her the next day. But then she died."

"What would you think if I told you that Alfredo wasn't

his real name? That he didn't own the villa but was a tour guide?"

"I'd think you were a stupid woman who didn't like to see other people happy. And I wouldn't care what he was. But then, at your age, you probably don't know a thing about true love."

"But I'm just trying to help," I started.

"I don't need your kind of help. Alfredo and I will help each other." She flounced out of the room.

I gathered the tea things and picked up the tray. I was starting to make sense of what had happened to Sally. I needed to act on it fast.

Before Caldwell could awaken from his nap and while everyone else had gone up to their rooms, I walked outside with my cell phone, called Inspector Blunderstone, and asked for his presence that night. After quizzing me, he agreed.

I leaned back against the side of the house and sighed. I hoped I was right.

THIRTY-FIVE

When Push Comes to Shove

I gathered everyone in the garden room, inviting them—one by one—there for refreshments. Everyone accepted with alacrity. They all seemed in need of a drink. Penelope took a small glass of white wine; Alfredo, a large glass of Campari; Bruce, a wine spritzer; Brenda said she wouldn't mind a taste of the wine; and I poured red wine for Caldwell and me.

Caldwell, still slightly befuddled from his nap, took the glass of wine I handed him and gave me a look that said, "What are you up to now?"

I kissed the tips of my fingers and put them gently on his lips, hopeful that I was saving him.

"Trust me," I said.

When the doorbell rang, I went to answer it and found the inspector standing there with a slight frown on his face.

"I hope you know what you're doing," he said.

"I do too."

I ushered him into the room and watched the faces of the gathered, noticing who looked more worried than surprised. What I saw strengthened my decision to go ahead with this private inquest.

Caldwell asked, "What brings you here? Are you going to take me away again?"

"You or someone else," the inspector said.

I could feel the tension in the room. Alfredo and Penelope moved closer together, Brenda wrung her hands, Bruce kept looking at the books on the low shelves, and Caldwell offered the inspector some wine.

"I'm on duty," he said.

"Of course you are," Caldwell agreed. "What is this all about, Karen? You seem to know what's going on."

The room became very still as everyone looked at me.

"Why don't we sit?" I suggested, thinking it would be easier to accuse someone of murder if they were all seated and it was done in a civilized manner.

As was only appropriate, Alfredo and Penelope took the love seat. Even after all I had told her about his subterfuge, they seemed to be holding together. Brenda perched on a stool near the fire. Bruce took what was usually Caldwell's chair, and Caldwell sat in a chair near me. The inspector leaned by the fire, and I stayed standing.

"I've been going over in my mind what happened to Sally and trying to figure out who would want her dead," I explained.

All eyes were boring into me. I took a big swallow of the red wine, hoping it would bolster my courage.

"I went over all the possible motives. Penelope, her sister, had always been jealous of Sally. Sally had even taken a precious ring Penelope had been given, just to tease her. And Penelope had fallen in love with Sally's boyfriend, Alfredo. Plus, she must have assumed, not knowing that Sally had changed her will, that she would get Sally's estate, if she died. She seemed to have the strongest reasons for killing her.

"Alfredo knew about the change of the will. Even though he told us otherwise. He had also fallen in love with Penelope, but had yet to tell Sally. If Sally died, he would get whatever Sally's estate was and Penelope.

"Caldwell, unfortunately, also had a good motive. Not that I thought him guilty for a moment. But he might certainly have done it for revenge and not wanting Sally to be able to claim any of the B and B."

By this time they were looking at one another as if trying to guess where I was going with this analysis.

"And lastly, I myself had an excellent motive. Maybe fearing that Sally would get some of the B and B and also claim Caldwell once again." I finished my glass of wine, preparing myself for the coup de grâce.

"Then, when I fell down the stairs this morning, I realized I was looking at the problem from the wrong direction. Sometimes a shock will do that to people, jolt them out of the box they're in."

Caldwell nodded at me to continue.

"So I saw that I was asking the wrong question. I was trying to figure out who might have wanted Sally dead, and suddenly I saw that the right question might be, Who were they really trying to kill?" I paused, then said, "It wasn't Sally."

Penelope's eyes grew wide, Alfredo murmured, *"Sacre bleu,"* Bruce stopped looking at the books and turned his attention to me, and Caldwell shook his head. I knew he would not like what I was about to say.

"Unfortunately—after I considered everyone—I saw that I was most likely the intended victim," I revealed.

Caldwell reached out and took my hand. "Karen?" he said.

I squeezed his hand and went on. "We all wondered what Sally was doing in the library that night. It was only by chance that the door was left open, and no one but Sally, who tried the door and got into the room, and I, who had left the door unlocked, knew this. So whoever saw someone in the room would have to assume it was either Caldwell or myself. Because who else would have the key?"

Stunned silence.

"Also, as I thought back to how Sally was dressed when we found her in the library, I remembered that she was wearing white night wear. I have a new white robe that Caldwell gave me when I arrived. So someone peeking into the library that night would see a woman wearing white and assume that it was me.

"I've come to the conclusion that Sally wasn't the intended victim, but I was." I watched as this statement made a ripple around the room. Bruce stood as if to leave, but Caldwell pushed him back down.

"Only two of you—other than Caldwell—knew that I had this robe. That would be Brenda and Bruce, who had both seen me wearing it from the days before Sally's demise.

"Then we come to motive. Who would want to kill me?

"I couldn't think why Bruce would want to kill me—unless his intention was not to kill me, but to create a diversion by knocking over the bookcase and, in the ensuing pandemonium, steal a valuable book that he was attempting unsuccessfully to buy from Caldwell. For a time I tried to believe this was true. It would have meant that no one was trying to kill anyone.

"But today I talked to Brenda and realized something." I

walked to where Brenda was sitting and pointed at her. "She was the one who killed Sally."

Brenda pushed me over and tried to make it to the door, but Caldwell grabbed her by the shoulders and swung her around, depositing her back in her chair. She collapsed, and the room exploded with everyone talking: Caldwell asking me if I was sure, Penelope and Alfredo finding themselves in each other's arms, the inspector on the alert in case Brenda tried to bolt again. Brenda, however, was sitting quite still.

Caldwell shook her shoulder and said, "Brenda? What do you have to say for yourself?"

Brenda stood up and said quietly, "She doesn't know what she's talking about. She's crazy."

Then her voice grew louder and higher as she turned to me. "You come in here and take over like you own the place. Well, Sally had much more right to be here than you."

Brenda had walked right into my trap. "Yes, that was the motive. Brenda was hoping if I was out of the picture that Sally might step back in and Caldwell and she could go back to being the happy family they once had been."

Brenda said, "You can't prove anything."

"You gave yourself away today, Brenda. I thought it might be you because of the similar white night wear and then because of the rolling pin you put on the stairs, hoping I would fall and break my neck. Which came from your domain—the kitchen. But after we talked today, I realized that when Sally died you were not downstairs in your bedroom as we had all assumed and as you said. You were actually upstairs, probably hiding in the bathroom after you had pushed over the bookcase."

"How do you know that?"

"You told me as much. When I suggested to you today that Caldwell might have done it, you said absolutely not. You said that you had heard him down in the kitchen. *Down*. If he was down, then you had to be upstairs. Which you were—pushing over the bookcase."

At this point, the inspector stepped in. He asked, "Is this true? Were you upstairs? Did you push over the bookcase?"

Brenda looked around, wild-eyed as a mink caught in a trap.

Then Bruce stepped in and said, "Yes, she was. I can confirm that she was upstairs. I walked into the library after most everyone was in there. But I looked back down the hallway as I went into the room, and I saw Brenda coming out of the upstairs bathroom. I didn't know it was important or I would have said something about it earlier."

The inspector took Brenda by the arm.

She shook him off. "But I didn't think the bookcase would kill anyone. I just wanted to throw a scare into Karen. Frighten her away. I wanted Sally to be back here. She was always so good to me. If that woman took Caldwell away and he sold the B and B, where would I be? Out in

the cold. I just wanted to hurt Karen. I didn't mean for anyone to die."

The inspector spoke to her in a clear and authoritative
voice. "You are under arrest for the murder of Sally Burroughs. It doesn't matter what you meant to do. This is an
obvious case of transferred malice."

THIRTY-SIX

With This Ring

"Transferred malice," Caldwell explained to me later that night, after the inspector had taken Brenda away, Alfredo and Penelope had announced they were going out for a quiet dinner, Bruce had gone up to his room to gloat over his books, and we two sat down to have another drink in the kitchen, "is a doctrine that states a person who intends to harm someone and then kills someone else in the process is guilty of murder."

"Oh," I said. "You are so smart."

"I looked it up on the Internet."

"But she'll be charged with murder?" I asked.

"We have to face facts. This is what happened. Brenda was trying to hurt you but instead killed Sally."

"Yes, but she didn't mean to *kill* me."

"No"—he reached out and grabbed my hand as if reassuring himself—"but if it had been you in there, hit by the falling bookcase, you might have died."

I drained my glass of wine and said, "I can't believe that. Somehow I don't think the books would have killed me. After all, I'm a librarian. I work with them every day."

Without asking he poured me another glass. "I won't argue with you about that. I think it's best you believe that books are your friends. But you figured out what happened to Sally and why."

"With your help. You gave me the piece about the rolling pin, telling me that it had been put in the wrong drawer."

"Yes, and I had been wondering about Brenda, but it was just so hard to believe. After all, she had been with me for such a long time. She was a good worker. I hope you don't mind if I say I will miss her."

"No, not at all. She didn't like me, but she did know how to keep this place clean. I'm not much of a housekeeper," I admitted.

"I'm neither disappointed nor surprised by this deficiency in you. I'm sure we can find someone else to do the work. That is not why I love you." He reached out for me, and I fell into his arms.

We kissed for a long time, standing by the table. Then I thought it might be best if we moved our embrace to a more intimate location.

"Let's go to bed. I'll collect the other glasses from the garden room," I said, and reluctantly pulled myself away.

"Okay, but the dishes can wait until morning," Caldwell said.

I heard voices as I walked down the hall. Taking a few more steps, I was able to see that Alfredo and Penelope were still sitting in the love seat, closer together than ever.

"But now I tell you the truth. You see, I am nothing," Alfredo said, raising his empty hands.

She pushed his hands down, taking hold of both of them. "There's nothing wrong with being a tour guide," Penelope said.

"I have no money."

"You'll surely get something from the B and B."

"But this place, the share of the B and B should be yours. Sally did not know what was in my heart. If she did . . ."

"I'm happy she left it to you."

"You mean this?" he asked.

"Yes, I didn't fall in love with you because you were rich or noble, I fell in love with you because you were you."

I stopped and watched as Alfredo slid off the love seat and onto the floor. Gracefully and on purpose. Down on one knee, he took Penelope's hand and said, "Please, I wish to marry you."

"Oh, *sì*," Penelope said.

"*Sì?*" he said.

"Yes, *sì*," she said.

He kissed her hand. Then he said, "But I have no ring."

Penelope reached into the pocket of her dress and pulled out the diamond and emerald ring. "But I do." She handed it to him.

He sat back down next to her and gently slipped the ring onto her finger. "It is beautiful, like you."

They kissed, and I decided to leave them alone.

For Penelope, Alfredo's love was enough. Maybe I could learn from her. I turned back down the hall. The glasses could certainly wait until morning.

THIRTY-SEVEN

What I Had to Do

Waking up the next morning, I knew what I had to do. If it was still possible. If I wasn't too late.

Caldwell was already downstairs, making tea and coffee, while I lollygagged. I jumped out of bed, threw on some clean clothes, which were getting harder to find, and ran down the stairs and almost knocked him over as he was carrying tea and toast to the garden room.

"Going somewhere?" he asked after we had kissed good morning.

"Actually, I am," I said.

"Time for tea?" he asked, continuing down the hall.

"Yes, please, but then I have to run."

He asked no questions. Another thing I loved about him. He didn't delve. He let me be. He trusted me to tell him when it was time.

I had some tea, kissed him on the cheek, and went out the door on my errand, still not telling him where I was going. I wanted it to be a surprise—if I could make it happen.

I walked the several blocks to the shop quickly, hoping that what I wanted was still there.

When I entered the store, I looked to where the pile of blankets had been, but there were only two left, and neither was the golden striped blanket that I had coveted. Disappointed, I walked farther into the store, hoping I still might find the special blanket tucked in another pile or draped over a chair. But I didn't see it anywhere.

The tall shopkeeper came out from behind her screen, her dark hair pulled back and fastened up high with two lacquer chopsticks.

"You're back," she said.

Surprised that she remembered me, I said, "Yes, but it looks like I'm too late."

"No, not quite. Another couple of days and you would have been. That's when I have to be out of the store. But I put the blanket aside for you."

"You did? It's still here?"

"Yes, I thought you might be back. And I decided if you weren't, I'd keep the blanket for myself."

She reached down under the counter and brought out the golden blanket with thin red stripes. The fabric was even more beautiful than I remembered it. The shopkeeper ran her hands over the wool.

"They don't make blankets like this anymore. A shame. For hundreds of years the tradition of weaving was strong in Wales, what with all the sheep. But now there's not many a mill left in the west."

"How old do you think this blanket is?"

"Oh, not quite an antique. I'd say mid–twentieth century."

Once again, I had to remember that what I thought was old was never very old by British standards. But then again, the blanket wasn't that much older than me. I ran my hand over the soft wool.

"Might I write the sale up for you?" she asked.

"Yes, absolutely. This is so kind of you to keep it for me. Why are you giving up the store?"

She laughed, and I could see how happy she was. "I got a better offer. I'm moving back to Wales to be with my guy. It's been a good run here, but I'm ready to leave London. I'd guess you'd say I'm retiring. Or traveling into another life. Feels good to be doing this."

"What's happening with this space?" I asked.

"I'm not sure. As far as I know, it isn't leased out yet,"

she said as she folded the blanket and put it in a large bag. "All I know is I will be out of here by the beginning of next month."

I looked around the brightly lit store. Not too large, about the size of two of Caldwell's garden rooms with what looked like more storage in the back. Not too small, the ceilings were at least twelve feet high, good for tall bookcases and maybe a rolling ladder. The space might be just right.

"That'll be eighty-nine pounds. Keep the receipt and you can get the VAT tax back when you leave," she told me.

I signed the slip she handed me and took the bag from her. "There's a chance I might not be leaving."

"Oh," she said, looking me over. "It would be nice if the blanket stayed in this country. And you too."

"Yes. Thank you, you've been so kind."

"Not at all. Just helping out a fellow traveler."

THIRTY-EIGHT

Just Right

When I tiptoed into Caldwell's bedroom, I saw him before he saw me. He was sitting in his reading chair, reading. He might not be the man of anyone else's dreams, but I was sure he was mine. Thoughtful, slightly wrinkled forehead; deep, drooping eyes; long fingers gently turning the pages; totally absorbed in a book.

Could I love him any more than I already did? I meant to find out.

"I bought us a blanket," I told him when he finally looked up at me.

"Us?" he asked hopefully.

I opened the bag and dumped the golden blanket in his lap. Then I spread it carefully over him. The blanket looked perfect.

"Yes, us," I said. "I've made up my mind. Since neither of us murdered Sally, so we're not going to jail, and we're in good health and I love you dearly and I think I might have found the perfect storefront for our shop, I thought all signs point to staying together."

Having said that, I plunked down on his lap on top of the blanket. He swaddled me in it and kissed me deeply and warmly. When he came up for air, he said, "You found a shop?"

"I think I did. Not far away. And it's just right—not too big, not too small. Also, it's where I bought this blanket."

"When can we see it?"

"Anytime. It will be vacant quite soon."

"You're amazing." Then he said, "Well, I have news for you too. I've decided to sell the book to Bruce."

I took his face in my hands. I knew this must have been a hard decision for him. A once-in-a-lifetime find. "You're sure? Your bunny book? But how can you part with it?"

"I think Bruce will enjoy it even more than me."

"It will certainly make him over-the-moon happy."

"Yes, so I will have the money for a down payment. And Penelope approached me this morning, after you'd left. She wants to buy me out of my share of the B and B. She and Alfredo are going to run this place together. They will focus on tours of London for people from Italy."

"What a great idea!" I said.

"And one last thing." He took my left hand gently in his. "My darling Karen, my librarian extraordinaire, would you marry me?" He held out a slim gold ring with a small diamond set between two even smaller rubies. "It was my mother's ring."

I held out my finger and let him slip it on. It fit perfectly.